BABY DRAMA III

(Baby Drama Series, Book 3)

SANDI LYNN

Sandi Lynn Romance, LLC

Baby Drama III

(Baby Drama Series, Book 3)

New York Times, USA Today & Wall Street Journal Bestselling
Author
SANDI LYNN

Mission Statement

Sandi Lynn Romance

Providing readers with romance novels that will whisk
them away
to another world and from the daily grind of life – one
book at a time.

Chapter One

CHARLIE

"This is how we're going to do it." I walked to my gate while on a Zoom call with my staff. "RIGHT!" I shouted, taking a seat. "We have thirty days until the game's launch, and it better be fixed. Do I pay you well enough? Do I give you all the time off you request? Do I pay for your health benefits? Do I give you gigantic yearly bonuses because you all deserve them?"

"Yes, Mr. Stone," my team spoke in unison.

"Exactly! So please give me the courtesy of fixing the fucking game before we launch it! Time's running out, people. Go! Get back to work and figure it out! I'll see you all tomorrow."

Sighing, I glanced at my watch. It was six p.m.

"Phew," I heard a woman's voice as she sat in the empty seat beside mine. "Yay!"

"Excuse me?" I glanced at her and was caught off-guard by her beauty.

"Oh, sorry. I was just upgraded to first class." She grinned, waving her boarding pass.

"Good for you." I smiled as I looked down at my phone.

"It's just I've never been in first class before."

"I'm sure you'll enjoy it." I read through my emails and tried to ignore her.

My phone rang, and I sighed when I saw it was Christine calling.

"Hello."

"I haven't heard from you since you left for Chicago," I noted the irritation in her voice. "I sent you some text messages, and you never responded."

"I've been busy, Christine. You know I'm here on business."

"Sure, Charlie. A friend there saw you out to dinner with a beautiful brunette. Was she part of your business?"

"As a matter of fact, she was, Christine. I'm not discussing this now or ever."

"I'm not either. Do me a favor, and don't ever call me again. I'm sick and tired of being disrespected by you. Do you understand me?" she shouted.

"Clearly, Christine. Thank you for making my day. Goodbye." I ended the call.

"Trouble in paradise?" the woman beside me asked, leaning closer.

"Excuse me?" I furrowed my brows.

"I couldn't help but overhear your phone call or the fact that your wife was shouting and accusing you of cheating on her."

"She is not my wife or girlfriend. There is no paradise, and therefore, there can be no trouble."

"Oh." She popped her lips.

"Do you always listen in on other people's phone conversations?" I asked.

"No."

"Then why were you listening in on mine?"

"I wasn't trying to, but when shouting is coming from the other end of the phone, it's kind of hard not to."

"Attention, passengers. Flight 2710 from Chicago to JFK has been delayed due to severe weather in New York City. We thank you for your patience and will keep you updated," I heard over the speaker.

"Shit," I sighed, shaking my head.

"Marley?" A man walked over with a wide grin.

"Oh, hey." She nervously smiled. "Are you on this flight?"

"Yeah. I just heard it was delayed. Want to go grab something to eat?" he asked.

"Uh, no. I'm good."

"Why not? We had fun last night." A smirk crossed the man's lips.

"Why are you making this weird?" She cocked her head.

"I'm not. It's just dinner. What is your problem?"

"I don't have a problem. I told you last night before I left not to make it weird."

"Asking you to stay the night was not making things weird," he said. "You know what? I think you're the weird one. The dinner invite is rescinded." He walked away.

"Okay, Trent. Who's the weird one?" she shouted.

"It's Troy!" He turned and glared at her.

"Oh. My bad."

"Wow." I chuckled.

"Shut up." Her brows furrowed.

I chuckled again as I looked down at my phone.

"I'm going to get a coffee. Can you save my seat?" she asked.

"I suppose I can," I spoke with irritation.

"Oh, I'm sorry. Is it too much of an inconvenience for you?" Her head cocked.

I stared into her baby-blue eyes as a smirk crossed my lips.

"No. Just hurry up and get me a medium Americano with an extra shot."

She stood up, staring at me with her hands on her hips.

"What?" I asked.

"I believe you forgot a word when you asked me to get you a coffee."

"No." I furrowed my brows. "Just a medium Americano with an extra shot."

"Did your parents ever teach you any manners? When you ask someone to get you something, you say 'please.'"

"Will you PLEASE get me a medium Americano with an extra shot!"

"I'll be right back. Make sure nobody steals my carry-on." She set her bag on her seat.

Sighing, I rolled my eyes and shook my head. Marley—strange name for a girl. She was a beautiful woman with long, lean legs who stood about five feet eight inches tall, with long blonde wavy hair, baby blue eyes, supple lips, a great body, and an attitude. But as beautiful as she was to look at, she was a little on the crazy side.

"Here you go." She handed me my Americano.

I took one sip and stared at her. "This isn't an Americano. It's just straight-up black coffee."

"They don't do Americanos where I went," she said, setting her carry-on on the floor and sitting down.

"There's a Starbucks right down there." I pointed. "Where did you go?"

"Starbucks was too far, and I'm tired."

"Did Troy keep you up all night? Oh, wait. That's

right. You left and told him not to make it weird." I chuckled.

"You're an asshole." She held out her hand.

"I know. What? Why are you holding out your hand?"

"You owe me six bucks for the coffee."

"Six dollars? Are you crazy? For this?" I held up my cup.

"I can't help what these places in the airport charge. I wasn't going to tell you about it, but since you didn't have the courtesy to say, 'Thank you,' I decided you would pay for your own coffee."

I pulled out my wallet, thumbed through my stack of bills, and handed her six dollars.

"Thank you." She smiled.

"Attention, passengers. Flight 2710 from Chicago to JFK will start boarding in five minutes." I heard over the speaker.

"Thank God." I let out a sigh of relief.

I wanted some peace, and I wasn't getting it with her sitting next to me. But as soon as I boarded the plane, I could finally relax.

"I have to use the restroom before we board," Marley said, grabbing her carry-on. "I'll see you on the plane. I'm assuming you're in first class, also?"

Shit.

"What gave it away?" A smirk crossed my lips.

"The designer suit, your cologne, and your arrogance." She began to walk away.

"Excuse me?!" I shouted, and she ignored me.

They called first class. I boarded the plane, put my bag in the overhead, sat in my seat, and brought up some articles I wanted to read on my phone.

"Looks like we're seatmates," I heard her voice.

Looking up, she stood there and shoved her carry-on into the overhead.

"Great," I mumbled.

"Did you say something?" She sat down. "Wow. Oh wow! These seats are so comfortable. I'm sorry, what were you saying?"

"Nothing." I let out a sigh.

Chapter Two

MARLEY

"A pillow? They actually give you a pillow in first class?" I grinned, holding it up.

"If you want to call it that," he said.

"What may I get you to drink before we take off?" The friendly flight attendant smiled at me. "We have coffee, soda, water, cocktails, wine."

"I'll have a glass of white wine, please."

"And for you, sir?"

"I'll have a scotch on the rocks. Listen, Marley. It is Marley?"

"Yes." I stared into his deep blue eyes.

"As enjoyable as it may be to talk to you, I have some articles I need to read."

"So, you want me to shut up and not talk to you?"

"Basically." He looked down at his phone.

The flight attendant walked over and handed us our drinks.

"Thank you." I sipped my wine. "It's fine." I glanced at him. "I'll leave you alone."

"I appreciate it," he spoke.

I wasn't going to lie. The man sitting in the seat next to mine was out of this world sexy. His six-foot-three stature, draped in a dark blue designer suit, possessed a commanding presence. His short dark hair framed his masculine features, and his piercing blue eyes were enough to catch anyone's attention. I wanted to reach over and run my fingers along the five o'clock shadow that made him even more handsome. But his arrogance and rudeness spoiled everything about him.

When we were at altitude, I stood up, opened the overhead, and grabbed my iPad from my carry-on.

"Excuse me. You're blocking the way, and I need to use the bathroom," Troy spoke with irritation.

"Sorry." I took my iPad and sat back in my seat.

As I was looking over my notes, Troy stopped at my seat on his way back from the bathroom.

"Can I help you?" I arched my brow, staring up at him.

"If you're from New York, you didn't mention that last night," he spoke nervously.

"You didn't ask," I said. "And you told me you lived in Chicago and were only staying in the hotel because your company paid for it when you attended a business conference."

"Don't think what happened last night will happen again. Got it?"

"Why are you making this weird?" I cocked my head. "It was one night."

"We're strangers, and we never met." He walked back to his seat.

The man next to me chuckled.

"Will you stop doing that?" I glanced at him.

"You slept with another woman's man." A smirk crossed his lips. "Either a wife, girlfriend, or fiancée."

"That is not true. I specifically asked him if he had a wife or girlfriend. He said no and that he was single."

He chuckled again. "Do you not know by now that men lie to get what they want?"

"Shit." I turned and saw him sitting two rows behind me in the aisle seat. Getting up, I walked over to him. "You have a girlfriend or a wife?" I spoke through gritted teeth, reaching down and gripping Troy's arm.

He swallowed hard and stared at me. "Yeah. I have a girlfriend back in New York. I didn't know you lived there too. Fuck."

"You're the epitome of a douchebag. I hope you're proud of yourself." I shook my head and went back to my seat.

"Told you." The cocky man next to me smiled.

"Shut up and go back to reading your articles."

God, I hated men sometimes.

We finally landed at JFK. Getting out of my seat, I grabbed my bag from the overhead and exited the plane. I couldn't wait to get home.

"You did nothing wrong," my seatmate said as he caught up with me. "He lied to you. That's on him."

"Thank you for your words of wisdom." I rolled my eyes as we stepped out of the airport.

"Enjoy the rest of your evening," he said, walking to the left.

I walked over to a cab that was waiting at the curb.

"You need a ride?" the driver asked.

"Yes, I do." I opened the door, threw my carry-on in the backseat, and climbed in.

"Where to, lady?" the cab driver asked.

"1022 Lexington Avenue."

My two best friends and roommates sat on the couch when I entered our apartment.

"It's about time," Olivia said, glancing at me.

"We missed you," Penelope said. "Get your ass over here." She patted the couch.

"I missed you guys too." I threw myself in between them.

"So, tell us about this guy who took you back to his hotel room last night. You bad, bad girl." Olivia grinned.

"Ugh." I threw my head back. "What a clusterfuck. First of all, the asshole lives here, in New York, and has a girlfriend, after he specifically told me he was single. Now, he's freaking the fuck out since we were on the plane together, in first class. That's right." A smirk crossed my lips. "First class."

"What? Girl, how did that happen?" Penelope asked.

"I was upgraded when I got to the airport. It was magical." I grinned. "Anyway, I met this other guy at the airport, and it turned out he was my seatmate."

"Name?" Olivia stared at me.

"I don't know," I said, twisting my face. "I didn't get his name. He was one of those guys you'd find in a GQ magazine. He looked like he just stepped right off the pages. But," I held up my finger, "underneath all that sexiness was rudeness and arrogance, which made him unsexy—sort of." I chewed my bottom lip.

"So now to the most important question," Penelope said. "Did you find the special fabric Mrs. Lake wants for the tablecloths?"

"I did. The store where I found it had just enough for all the tables. They're making the tablecloths and will overnight them by the end of next week. Now, all I need to do is go to the florist and have the arrangements made."

"And how much is this five-year-old birthday bash costing?" Olivia asked.

"Seventy-five thousand dollars." I rolled my eyes.

"Oh, Marley." Penelope placed her hand on my shoulder. "We need your help." She pouted.

"We had to fire timid little Ingrid," Olivia said.

"Why?"

"She couldn't keep all the coffees straight and kept screwing up orders. We had too many complaints, and the last thing we need is bad reviews."

"I can give you time in between event prepping."

"We'll take anything." Penelope hugged me.

"Thanks, Marley. We knew we could count on you." Olivia hugged me. "We'll start interviewing soon."

Penelope and Olivia were my other halves; we had been inseparable since we were ten. We did everything together—cried together, laughed together, and were always there for each other through the good times and the bad.

Penelope was beautiful with her five-foot-six stature, long auburn colored hair, and green eyes. Olivia was equally stunning with her ebony skin, five-foot-eight slender body, high cheekbones, and rich chocolate eyes. We grew up on Long Island, and after we graduated high school, we backpacked around Europe before heading to NYU and having to become adults.

Two months ago, Olivia and Penelope became the proud owners of Love At First Sip, a trendy coffee shop they always discussed opening. Their parents gave them seed money, and the rest came from the bank. They wanted me to join their little venture, but my passion lay in event planning. That was who I was—a planner—ever since my life fell apart at the tender age of eleven.

Chapter Three

CHARLIE

"Just set the boxes on the floor according to the room," I told the movers as they unloaded their truck.

"Damn, Charlie. Look at this place. You have really outdone yourself, my friend." Chase, my best friend and president of my company, smiled. "When you first showed me this place, I wasn't sure. The décor, the walls, and everything about it sucked. Adalyn Grant transformed this place into a bachelor's palace."

"Thanks." I chuckled, handing my friend a scotch. "She did excellent work." I held up my glass.

"That she did." Chase tipped his glass to mine. "But, why so big for a man who never plans to marry or have children? I mean, come on. What does a bachelor who is never getting married or having children need with all this space?"

"I love the layout, the location, and it was a hell of a steal. I wasn't about to turn away from it just because it has five bedrooms and five bathrooms."

"Yeah, I guess. I probably wouldn't have either."

"Besides." I grinned, placing my hand on his shoulder. "You'll always have a room here for when Lila kicks your ass out. But first, I'll need to buy an extra bed." I smirked.

"Thanks." He rolled his eyes. "You're going to have some good, sexy times in this palace. Speaking of. What happened with Christine? We really haven't had a chance to talk since you returned from Chicago."

"She's nuts." I tipped the glass to my lips. "She called me while I was at the airport going on about how I didn't call or text her during my whole two-day trip and wanted to know who the beautiful woman was I had dinner with."

"Was she talking about your cousin Meg?" His brow arched.

"Yes. Then she told me she was sick and tired of my disrespecting her and to never call her again."

"What is with women always saying the exact same thing to you?" Chase asked.

"Who the hell knows, and who the hell cares. We've only been seeing each other on and off for three months. The last night we were together, she commented about my meeting her parents and how she felt it was time."

"Shit. That's enough to make the great Charlie Stone run in the opposite direction." He chuckled.

"I was going to tell her I didn't want to see her anymore when I got back, but she saved me the trouble. I want to show you something. Follow me."

I led him down the hallway and opened the six-panel white double doors.

"What the fuck!" Chase exclaimed as we stepped into my office/gaming room.

"My bachelor pad is now a three-bedroom, four-bathroom home," I grinned. "I had the wall knocked down between the bedrooms and removed the bathroom."

"I can't believe you didn't tell me about this, Charlie.

This is awesome. I may have to start picking fights with Lila, so she'll kick me out."

I laughed. "Let's test out our new game system."

We sat on the Italian leather recliner couch that faced the 150-inch TV hung on the wall. After testing our new game system, I walked over to the bar and poured another drink.

"This system will blow out every Nintendo, Sony, and Xbox out there. We're talking millions, baby." Chase's face glowed.

"I hope so. I kind of met this woman at the Chicago airport."

"Oh? Do tell."

"Her name is Marley."

"That's a cool name," Chase said.

"She's weird."

"What do you mean?" He laughed.

"I don't know. She's a beautiful woman but weird. She told me I was arrogant."

"You are." He shrugged.

"Shut the fuck up. She had a one-night stand in Chicago with some guy. He ended up on our flight, and when he tried to talk to her, she kept asking him why he was making it weird."

"Making what weird?" Chase tipped the glass of scotch to his lips.

"I guess the fact they had sex, and he was trying to talk to her. Anyway, it turns out he lives here in New York and has a girlfriend."

"That bastard." He smiled. "What does this Marley girl do?"

"I have no clue. I didn't ask."

"Where in the city does she live?"

"No idea. She was driving me nuts, so I told her I had articles to read and to stop talking."

"If she drove you nuts, why are you telling me about her?" A smirk crossed his lips.

"I don't really know. Maybe because she was beautiful and very opinionated. I don't know." I let out a sigh. "I wouldn't have minded fucking her as long as she kept her mouth shut."

"You're such a douchebag." Chase laughed, pulling his phone from his pocket. "That was Lila. I have to go."

"You're so pussy-whipped."

"What can I say? That's what love does to a man. Not that you'd know anything about that." He patted my shoulder as we walked out of the room.

"And I never will, my friend. I'll see you tomorrow at the office."

After Chase left, I stood in the middle of the kitchen and stared at the boxes that still needed to be unpacked.

"CHARLIE, Preston is here to see you." My assistant, Julia, opened my office door.

"Send him in. By the way, I need you to go to my new penthouse, unpack the boxes in the kitchen, and get everything put away. Take one of the interns with you to help."

"Okay. I'll go now."

Preston walked into my office with a disc in his hand.

"We fixed it, Charlie." He handed me the disc.

"You're sure this time?" My brow arched.

"Yeah." He smiled.

"Thank you. I'll test it out now."

I slipped the disc into the game system, sat on the

leather couch, and began playing. My office door opened, and Chase walked in.

"Did they fix it?" he asked.

"It appears they did." I smiled.

"We need to leave for that meeting now with Walsh Software," he said.

"Shit. I forgot about that." I shut the game off, grabbed my suitcoat, and we left the office.

"After our meeting, I want to stop at this coffee shop. It's right near where our meeting is," Chase said.

"Why?"

"Lila keeps talking about it. She said they have the best coffee—better than Starbucks."

"What's this place called?" I asked.

"Love At First Sip. Cute, right?" He grinned.

After our meeting ended, I had my driver, Mateo, take us to Love At First Sip. When we stepped inside, I stopped dead in my tracks when I saw the barista behind the counter.

"What's wrong?" Chase turned his head.

"That's her."

"Who?"

"Marley. The beautiful woman from the airport."

Chapter Four

MARLEY

I stood behind the counter, taking orders while Olivia made the coffee drinks, and Penelope was in the back interviewing someone. The place was hopping, and I saw *him* when I looked up to see how long the line was. My heart started racing at an uncontrollable speed.

When it was his turn, he and another man approached the counter.

"Well, if it isn't my seatmate." A smirk crossed his lips.

"Let me guess. A medium Americano with an extra shot." I smiled.

"You remembered."

"I have a good memory. And what can I get for you?" I asked his friend.

"Same as him."

"You didn't tell me you were a barista."

"That's because you told me to stop talking to you." I smirked. "Besides, you never told me your name."

"It's Charlie." His friend grinned.

"Charlie." I picked up a Sharpie with a smile and wrote his name on the cup.

"And you are?"

"Chase, his best friend."

"Chase." I wrote his name on the cup.

Charlie pulled some cash from his wallet and handed it to me.

"Thank you. Your coffees will be up right over there. Have a great day!" I brightly grinned.

"You too." His eye slightly narrowed at me as the corners of his mouth lifted.

As soon as their coffees were made, they took them to a table and sat down.

"I saw you flirting with that one in the dark suit. He's delicious looking." Olivia smiled.

"That's the man I met at the airport."

"Oh? The sexy but arrogant one?"

"Yep." I popped my lips.

"Arrogant or not, I'd totally hit that." She grinned.

"He thinks I work here." I glanced at her.

"Did you tell him you don't and are only filling in?"

"Nah. Why bother? Since the rush is over, I need to leave. You don't mind, right? I have to get to the florist and order the floral arrangements for the party."

"Go ahead."

"Great news!" Penelope walked from the back. "Myron, I'd like you to meet my business partner, Olivia, and our best friend/sister, Marley. Girls, meet our new barista."

After saying hi, I grabbed my purse and walked over to where Charlie and Chase sat.

"It was nice to see both of you. My shift ended, and I'm leaving."

Charlie glanced at his watch. "It's only noon. How is your shift over already?"

"Short shift. Bye." I smiled, turned around, and walked out the door.

∽

One Week Later

"HI, Myron. How do you like working here so far?" I asked as I walked into the coffee shop.

"I love it. It's the perfect part-time job while I'm in college." He smiled.

"And we love having him here." Penelope hooked her arm around him.

"Are you going to tell her?" Olivia looked at Penelope.

"Tell me what?" I cocked my head.

"That guy you met at the Chicago airport was in here this morning," Penelope said.

"He wanted to know if you were working." Olivia smiled.

"He asked that?"

"His exact words were, 'Is Marley, the barista, working today?'" Penelope spoke in a manly voice.

"We told him that it was your day off. He looked disappointed," Olivia said.

"Day off? I don't even work here." I laughed.

"So what?" Olivia shrugged. "I think he wants to ask you out. Next time he comes in, we'll give him your phone number."

"Don't you dare. I'm on a sex/dating hiatus." I pointed at them.

"Since when?" Penelope's brows furrowed.

"Since that asshole in Chicago."

"Oh my God, I forgot to tell you girls. My cousin invited us to a party tonight. Her boss is throwing it. I guess he just moved into some fancy-ass penthouse and is having a housewarming party," Penelope said.

"Where is her boss's penthouse?" I asked.

"133 East 73rd Street."

"That's right by where we live," I said.

"Exactly. We could walk. Say you'll come. It'll be fun. I've never been to a penthouse party before," Penelope begged.

"You know I'm in." Olivia grinned.

"I guess I'll go." I smiled. "But I can't stay late. I have to be up early tomorrow morning and make sure everything is ready and set for the Lake's party on Sunday."

"WHICH ONE?" I asked my girls, holding up two short black dresses.

"That one." They both pointed to the left.

My phone rang. Walking back to my bedroom, I grabbed it from the bed and saw my mother was calling.

"Hey, Mom."

"Why haven't I heard from you?" she asked.

"I've been swamped planning an extravagant party for a five-year-old, Mom."

"It doesn't matter, Marley. You should make time to call your mother. I'm cooking dinner Sunday and would like you to join us."

"I can't. I'm working all day."

"On a Sunday?" she asked with irritation.

"Yes, Mom. The party I've been planning for months is on Sunday. We'll have to do dinner another time."

"I haven't seen you in almost two months. And the last

time I was in the city, you weren't answering your phone and nowhere to be found."

"I told you I was working that day. Mom, I have to go. I'm getting ready to go out."

"We'll set something up for next week. Have fun tonight."

Sighing, I threw my phone on the bed and slipped into my short black fitted dress.

"You can't avoid her forever, Mar," Penelope said, standing in the doorway, holding a bottle of whiskey.

"I'm not avoiding her."

"You are. Can I borrow those cute hoop earrings you have?" Olivia asked, walking over to my jewelry box.

"Sure. And I am not avoiding her. I think once every three months or so is enough visiting time."

"At some point, you have to forgive her and your dad," Penelope said.

"No, she doesn't. If my parents did what they did, I'm not sure I'd ever forgive them." Olivia placed the earrings in her ears.

I grabbed my black heels from the closet. As I walked past Penelope, I grabbed the whiskey from her hand and brought the bottle to my lips, taking a large sip.

"Come on, my sisters. Let's go to this penthouse party and have some fun." I grinned.

Chapter Five

CHARLIE

Servers walked around with trays of champagne and appetizers while I greeted my guests.

"Hey, Charlie." Kyra, one of my interns, smiled, walking over to me.

"Hi, Kyra. Thanks for coming."

"I hope you don't mind, but I invited my cousin. The problem is I didn't know she'd bring her two best friends. Well, I should have known since they're attached at the hip. I'm sorry," she whined. "I just wanted my cousin to meet you."

"It's fine, Kyra. Don't worry about it. Go and enjoy the party."

I glanced over and saw Chase and Lila step off the elevator.

"Wow, Charlie. Look at this place." Lila smiled as I kissed her cheek.

"Thanks, Lila. I'll have Chase give you the grand tour."

"I can't wait to show her your gaming room." Chase grinned.

"You boys and your toys." Lila smirked.

"Excuse me, wife, but those toys let us live the luxury lifestyle we do." Chase's brow arched at her.

I laughed. "Go grab some champagne and show her the room." I patted Chase's back.

As I was walking away from the elevator, I heard it ding. Turning around, I couldn't believe my eyes.

"Marley?" My brows furrowed.

"Oh, hey, Charlie." She grinned. "Fancy seeing you here. You also work for Penelope's cousin's boss?"

"Something like that." I smiled.

"These are my best friends, Penelope and Olivia."

"It's nice to meet both of you." I shook their hands.

"Wow. Check out these digs." Olivia scanned the place. "Oh, I see champagne. Come on, girls." She grabbed Marley's and Penelope's hand."

"I guess I'll talk to you later." Marley smiled.

A smile graced my lips as I watched Marley being dragged away by her best friends. I couldn't believe she was here.

"Uh, did I just see Marley, the barista?" Chase walked over.

"You sure did."

"What the hell is she doing here? Did you invite her?"

"No. I'm guessing she's the friend of Kyra's cousin." I tipped the glass of scotch to my lips.

"I seriously can't believe Kyra would invite people to your party," Chase said. "That was really ballsy of her."

"In this case, I'm happy she did." I smirked.

I couldn't stop staring at her as she stood in the middle of my penthouse, sipping champagne and talking with her friends. Pouring myself a glass of scotch, I walked over to where she stood.

"Having a good time?" I asked.

"Yeah, I am." She smiled. "This place is really cool. So, which rich guy here is the homeowner? I'd like to personally compliment him on his fabulous living space."

"Ah." Kyra walked over. "I see you girls have met my boss, Charlie Stone."

The corners of my mouth curved upward as I stared at Marley. She cocked her head with an arch in her brow.

"You? You live here? This is your party? You're Kyra's boss?"

"Yes. Yes. Yes. And yes."

"You own Stone Game Ventures?" Her eyes narrowed.

"I do." A smile crossed my lips. "Do you like to play video games?"

"I do, sometimes." She smiled.

"Good to know." I winked and walked away.

MARLEY

I swallowed hard as I could feel the heat rise throughout my body.

"That man wants you, girl," Olivia said.

"Stop it." I blushed. "He does not."

"The hell he doesn't," Penelope said. "Did you see the way his sexy eyes stared into yours? Even I was mesmerized."

"Welp, it's too bad our girly here is on a dating/sex hiatus." Olivia smirked, hooking her arm around me.

"Yeah. Too bad." I tipped the glass to my lips.

"I bet he has a king-size bed and performs outstandingly in it," Olivia said.

"Stop it." I put my hand up.

"Why?" she whispered in my ear. "Is Moaning Marley ready to come out and play?"

"Oh, my God! Knock it off." I playfully smacked her arm.

"You know you want to see what's going on under those fine pants he's wearing," Penelope said.

"I bet it's HUGE," Olivia said.

"And thick," Penelope added.

"You two need to stop right now!" I pointed. "I bet it is, too." I grinned.

"Ha! We knew it." Olivia laughed.

When the server walked over asking if we'd like another glass of champagne, we each snagged another glass. As I slowly sipped it, I stared at Charlie from across the room.

"I need some fresh air," I said to the girls.

I stepped onto the terrace and rested my arms against the railing, staring out into the brightly lit city of New York. Suddenly, I felt a hand on my lower back.

"Enjoying the view?" Charlie's voice spoke.

"I am." I glanced at him.

"Me too." He smirked. "Have I told you how beautiful you look tonight?"

"Just tonight? Not the other times we've run into each other?" My brow arched. I rendered him speechless and laughed. "Just kidding. Thank you for the compliment."

"To answer your question, no, not just tonight."

"Thanks." I blushed. "You do have a really nice home. The décor is beautiful. Did you decorate it yourself?"

"No. I hired Adalyn Grant to help me."

"She's one of the most sought-after interior designers in New York." I smiled.

"She and her husband Harrison are good friends of mine."

"Nice." I held up my glass.

"Your glass is almost empty. Can I get you another?"

"Sure. Why the hell not?" A smile crossed my lips.

"Let's go inside, and I'll pour you something a little stronger."

We walked back inside the penthouse, and Charlie had to say goodbye to some guests before he poured me another drink. I was already feeling the effects of the glasses of champagne I consumed and wasn't sure if drinking anything else was smart.

"We saw you talking to Mr. McBillionaire out there." Penelope smiled, grabbing my hand.

"Attention, everyone," Charlie spoke, standing in the middle of the room. "I want to thank everyone for coming tonight. I hope you all had a good time. Speaking of the time," he glanced at his watch, "the party is over."

"Who does that?" Olivia snarled in my ear. "Who just kicks everyone out of their party?"

"Billionaires who've had enough?" I shrugged.

"Come on, girls. Let's continue this party at home." Penelope grinned.

"Let me say goodbye to Charlie," I said, walking over to where he stood. "Thanks for having us. It was fun."

"Are you leaving already?" he asked.

"Well, yeah. You just announced the party was over."

"I didn't mean for you and your friends. I do believe I still owe you a drink." A smile crossed his lips.

"We should really go."

"Or you can stay and do some shots with us." Chase hooked his arm around me. "Right, Lila?"

"Yeah. Stay. It'll be fun with just us."

"Okay. Why not?" I smiled.

After the last of the guests left, Chase walked over to the bar and grabbed a bottle of tequila.

"Tequila shots, anyone?" He grinned, holding up the bottle.

"Yeah!" We girls shouted.

"I'll get out the salt and limes." Charlie smiled.

We gathered around the island and did shots of tequila.

"Let's dance!" Lila shouted, putting on the song Truth Hurts by Lizzo.

The four of us started wildly dancing around the living room, jumping up and down and twerking while singing the song.

Chapter Six

CHARLIE

"Get it, girl!" Chase shouted at Lila. "Damn, I'm the luckiest man in the world."

I stood there and watched Marley dance around the room. My cock was twitching and aching to be inside her. That body of hers was enticing, and with any luck, she'd be in my bed all night, letting me do very bad things to her. I was feeling the effects of all the alcohol I'd drunk throughout the night. I never was one to mix alcohol, but tonight I did.

The song ended, and Lila fell into Chase's arms.

"Take me home and take me to bed, you sexy knight." She drunkenly smiled at Chase.

"It's been fun, Charlie, but I have to go." Chase grinned, swooping Lila up in his arms. "I'll talk to you tomorrow. Ladies, it was great fun meeting all of you."

"Night, Chase," Marley said.

"I guess we better go," Olivia said.

"Can I call you a cab?" I asked.

"Nah, we just live around the block. I need the fresh air," Penelope said.

I reached over and grabbed Marley's hand. "I want you to stay."

Her beautiful eyes stared into mine. "Uh—"

"She's on a sex hiatus," Penelope blurted out. "Come on, Mar."

"A sex hiatus?" I cocked my head at her. "Since when?"

"Since Trent in Chicago," Marley spoke with seriousness.

"You mean Troy." I chuckled.

"Right." She held up her finger. "I think I'll stay for a while. I'll see you girls later."

"You have to be up early tomorrow morning," Penelope said. "And as your besties, we—"

"Leave her alone," Olivia hooked her arm around Penelope. "If she wants to stay, let her stay. Fuck her hiatus. Don't be stumbling through the door and waking our asses up." Olivia pointed at her.

"I'll make sure she gets home safely," I said. "Goodnight, ladies. Those are some great friends you have there."

"Yeah. They're the best. How about another shot of tequila?"

"Are you sure?" I asked.

"Yep. One hundred percent." A beautiful grin crossed her face.

I poured us another shot. That last one did me in. I couldn't remember the last time I was this drunk.

I gripped Marley's hips and lifted her up on the island. Her legs wrapped around my waist.

"The things I want to do to you," I said, staring into her eyes.

"The things I want you to do to me." She drunkenly smiled.

I couldn't resist her anymore. Smashing my mouth into hers, our kiss was wild. My hand traveled up her dress until my fingers reached the edge of her panties.

"Fuck," I moaned, dipping a finger inside.

"Bed. Bed. I need to lay down," she said.

I lifted her from the island, carried her to my bedroom, and lay her down.

MARLEY

Opening my eyes, everything was blurry, and my head was pounding out of control. Glancing over, I saw him lying there, on his stomach, with his muscular back exposed and the sheet covering half of his perfect ass.

"Oh, fuck!" I quickly sat up and covered myself with the sheet.

Charlie moaned, rolling over and opening his eyes.

"Good morning."

"Did we?" I stared at him, but I already knew the answer.

"Multiple times." A sly grin crossed his lips.

I glanced at the clock, and it was eleven-thirty. "Oh shit!" I jumped out of bed.

"What's wrong?"

"It's eleven thirty. I have to go." I grabbed my panties from the floor.

"Why?" Charlie asked.

"I have a lot of things to do today. Oh my God. I can't believe I slept this late." I grabbed my dress and slipped it on.

"Marley—"

"Don't." I pointed at him. "Don't make this weird, Charlie."

He chuckled.

"What is so funny?" I asked, running into the bathroom to check out how much of a disaster I looked like. I grabbed his hairbrush from the counter and ran it through my hair.

"The fact that you remembered my name."

"You're a jerk." I pointed at him as he lay there smiling.

I ran to the living room and grabbed my heels while Charlie followed.

"Can I at least make you a cup of coffee before you sprint out of here?"

"No! It was just sex. Don't make it weird."

"I'm not." His brows furrowed.

"Yes. Yes, you are." I pushed the elevator button.

"Marley, you're forgetting something."

I turned and saw Charlie holding up my purse.

"Ugh. Thanks." I grabbed it from him and stepped into the elevator.

"I'll see you around sometime," he said as the doors closed.

I raced out of the building, holding my shoes in one hand and holding the other up, yelling for a taxi. When one finally stopped, I climbed into the back, and the driver stared at me.

"Rough night?"

"None of your business." I gave him the address to where I needed to be. "I need you to step on it, please."

Pulling out my phone, I Facetimed Olivia.

"Good lord, Marley." Penelope's face appeared.

"Is that her?" I heard Olivia's voice in the distance.

"I thought you were coming home last night?" Penelope said.

"I don't really remember last night. I woke up in Charlie's bed at eleven thirty."

Olivia grabbed the phone, and her face appeared on the screen.

"You're actually going out in public looking like that. You look like you've been fucked senseless and every which way."

"Shh!" I said, looking up and noting the cab driver staring at me through the rearview mirror. "I'm only calling because I didn't want you two to worry."

"Oh, we weren't worried. We knew you were in good hands with Charlie McBillionaire." Olivia smirked.

"So tell us." Penelope smiled. "How were his hands all over your body?"

"Goodbye!" I ended the call.

I pulled the compact from my purse and tried to wipe the mascara stains from under my eyes.

The cab driver pulled up to the curb of the florist.

"Please, wait for me. I won't be long." I opened the door.

"It's your money." He smiled.

The bell above the door, which I always thought was so cute, annoyed the hell out of me today. Stepping inside the shop, I looked around for Miguel.

"You're late, Marley. Oh, my. What is this?" Miguel walked over and studied me, bringing his finger to his lips.

"Do not, and I mean, do not judge me." I pointed at him.

"I've never seen you look like such a hot mess before," he said, hooking his arm around mine. "Do tell me what happened last night. Because judging by this look, you had a wild time."

"I drank too much, slept with a billionaire, and woke

up late. Now that you have all the details, show me the arrangements."

"You're going to love them." He grinned. "Come in the back."

I stared at the centerpieces, which were little pink tutus made of tulle, with pink and white roses in the center and sprigs of baby's breath.

"Adorable." I smiled. "Mrs. Lake will love them. Make sure they're delivered to the house tomorrow at nine a.m."

"Delivery is already set up, darling. Now, tell me about this billionaire you bedded last night." A sly grin crossed his face.

Chapter Seven

CHARLIE

Reaching into the cabinet, I shook two aspirins in my hand and chased them down with a bottle of water. I hadn't been this hungover in a long time. Climbing into the hot shower, I let the soothing water beat down me as I thought about Marley. Last night was great—at least, the parts I could remember.

After showering and dressing, I made the bed. Grabbing the used condom from my nightstand, I threw it in the trash can and looked on the floor around the bed for the others. Shit. Getting down on my knees, I looked under the bed and didn't see any. I knew for a fact we had sex three times last night. How was there only one condom? Walking back into the bathroom, I picked up the trashcan and looked in it, noting the one condom I'd just thrown in there. Shit.

I heard the elevator ding, and my cleaners stepped into the foyer with their cleaning supplies.

"Good morning, Mr. Stone." Greta smiled.

"Good morning, Greta. Good morning, Sylvia."

"Morning." Sylvia scanned the mess.

"I'm heading to the office. I'll be gone for a few hours. I left an envelope on the island with your money, plus a bonus for the extra mess."

"Always appreciated, Mr. Stone," Greta spoke.

When I arrived at the office, I sat behind my desk, turned on my computer, and turned my chair around to stare out at the busy city.

"Knock. Knock," I heard Chase's voice.

"What are you doing here?" I asked, turning my chair around.

"I forgot the Bradshaw file on my desk. I want to review it again before our meeting on Monday."

"Ah, good idea," I said.

"Don't forget about that birthday party tomorrow we have to go to," Chase said, sitting across from my desk.

"What birthday party?" My brows furrowed.

"For Derek Lake's five-year-old daughter. For fuck's sake, Charlie. Don't tell me you forgot."

"Shit." I ran my hand down my face. "Why do we have to go? The last way I want to spend my Sunday is at a birthday party with God knows how many children running around screaming."

"You know why." He pointed at me. "He invited us, and we need to close this deal."

"Do I have to bring a gift?" I asked.

"Really, Charlie?" He cocked his head. "I'm sure Julia already bought it. Text her."

Grabbing my phone, I sent my assistant a text message.

"Did you buy a gift for Derek Lake's little girl's birthday party?"

"Yes. I told you I did two weeks ago. It's in your office closet, all wrapped and ready to go."

"Thank you, Julia."

"No problem, Charlie."

I stood up from my desk, opened the closet door, and pulled out the large pink bag with little ballerinas all over it. Shaking my head, I set it on the floor next to my desk.

"Do we really have to—"

"Yes!" Chase chuckled. "Now, tell me about last night after Lila and I left."

"What do you think happened?" I smirked.

"And?"

"I'm concerned about something," I sighed.

"What?"

"From what I can remember, we had sex three times before we passed out. When I got up this morning, I could only find one used condom."

"Shit, Charlie. Are you sure?"

"Yes, I'm sure. I looked everywhere."

"I wouldn't worry about it. I'm positive that a girl like Marley is on birth control."

"What do you mean by 'a girl like Marley?'"

"Well, I think she probably sleeps around. You said she slept with that guy in Chicago. She's definitely on birth control. But don't be so stupid next time, my friend. So, when she left this morning, how did the two of you leave things?"

"She flew out of bed because she was late for something. Then she told me I was making things weird."

Chase laughed.

"I don't think she remembers us having sex."

"Why do you think that?" His brows furrowed.

"Because when she woke up in a panic, she asked if we did. That last shot of tequila we did after you left did us in."

"Ah, the tequila shame." He grinned. "Do you like her?"

"I don't even know her."

"Did you get her phone number?" he asked.

"No. She flew into the elevator like a madwoman."

"Do you want to see her again?" His brow arched.

"I don't know. I got what I wanted last night. I think it's best we leave it at that."

"I like her." He smiled. "And so does Lila."

"Okay? Then you and Lila date her." I smirked.

"Will you ever grow up and get serious with someone?" Chase stood up from his seat.

"Nope." I smiled. "My life is as good as it gets. Besides, emotions aren't my thing. I've been on my own for a very long time, and that's how I like it. I don't need women drama in my life. Look at Christine."

"And Kara, Claire, Suzanne, Scarlet, Jenny—need I go on?" His brow arched.

"No. You can stop." I stood up from my desk.

"You're a manwhore, Charlie Stone." Chase grinned. "I'll see you tomorrow at Derek's house. Don't be late."

After I left the office, I took a cab and had the driver drop me off across the street from Love At First Sip. Why? I hadn't a clue. I stood with my hands tucked into my pants pockets and stared from the street at the patrons walking into the shop. I could see two baristas behind the counter through the large window. Neither was Marley.

"What the hell am I doing?" I whispered to myself.

I hailed a cab and headed home. When I stepped off the elevator, a fresh, clean scent radiated throughout the spotless space. After changing my clothes, I headed to Club Luxe to meet my friend Brian for a few drinks.

Chapter Eight

MARLEY

I grabbed my ringing phone from the counter and saw my assistant, Tami, was calling.

"Hey, Tam."

"Ugh, Marley. I'm so sorry to do this, but I can't work tomorrow." Her voice sounded horrible.

"Tami, what's wrong?" I asked in a panic.

"I just got back from Urgent Care, and I have strep throat. I'm so sorry. Will you be able to find someone to help you?"

I glanced at the couch where Olivia and Penelope sat watching Sex And The City.

"Yeah, I'll get someone. Feel better."

"Thanks, Marley. I'm really sorry."

"Don't be. You take care of yourself."

Walking over to the couch, I squeezed in between my two best friends and hooked my arms around their necks.

"So, which one of you is helping me with the party tomorrow?"

"What happened to Tami?" Penelope asked.

"She just called. She has strep throat."

"Oh hell no," Olivia said. "You know me and kids don't mix."

"Well, I have that baby shower I HAVE to go to for my cousin, Thea. You know I can't miss it, or my mom will kill me," Penelope said.

"Looks like it's you." I smiled, kissing the side of Olivia's head.

"I'm putting it out there now. I am in no way responsible for what I may say or do in front of those kids."

"You'll have fun." I grinned. "It's a ballerina party."

Olivia stuck her finger down her throat and acted like she was going to vomit.

THE FOLLOWING MORNING, Olivia and I loaded the boxes for the candy table in my car.

"Is this it?" she asked as we put in the last box.

"Yeah. Everything else is already arranged." I glanced at my watch. "We have to leave now. I don't want to be late and have Mrs. Lake up my ass. Her anxiety is through the roof as it is."

We climbed into my car and drove to Brooklyn, arriving at the Lake's townhome with five minutes to spare.

"Are you still thinking about Charlie McBillionaire?" Olivia asked, pulling a box from the back of the car.

"No. And I never was thinking about him," I lied.

"Yeah, right." She laughed. "He lives around the block from us. Walk over and say hi."

"No. What is wrong with you?" My brows furrowed.

The front door flew open, and Mrs. Lake ran down the steps.

"Marley, thank God you're here. We have a problem."

"What's wrong, Mrs. Lake?"

"The floral arrangements are all wrong!"

"Impossible. I saw them yesterday. Miguel did an excellent job."

"No. Hurry up and get inside, and I'll show you." She flew up the concrete steps.

"I have no idea how you put up with these people." Olivia shook her head.

Stepping into the monstrous townhome, I set the box down and walked over to the table where the centerpieces were sitting.

"Mrs. Lake, they're beautiful."

"Marley, they're all wrong. I wanted a white ribbon around the tutus, not pink!"

Was she serious?

Taking my phone from my purse, I pulled up the notes I had taken.

"Mrs. Lake, you said you wanted pink ribbon." I held my phone up.

"Why would I want that? The white stands out more. You misheard me."

"No. I did not mishear you." I shook my head.

"You want my honest opinion?" Olivia walked over.

"I'm sorry. Who are you?" Mrs. Lake asked.

"I'm Olivia, Marley's friend and assistant for today. The white ribbon would have taken away from the entire look of the centerpiece." Olivia looked around and grabbed one of the balloons with a white ribbon string. She wrapped the ribbon around the centerpiece. "See, when you look at the centerpiece, the only thing your eyes focus on is the white ribbon. You don't want that, Mrs. Lake. You want your guests to focus on the beautiful roses and the cute little tutus."

"Oh. I suppose you're right."

"That's why you said pink ribbon because you already knew that. You just forgot," Olivia said.

"Then I guess we don't have an issue." Mrs. Lake smiled at me. "I'll let you ladies get things set up while I finish getting ready."

"Thanks." I glanced at Olivia.

"That woman needs a Xanax. Let's get the rest of the boxes from the car."

The entire party was ballerina-themed. Mrs. Lake's five-year-old daughter, Sadie, loved ballet, so all the little girls who attended the party had to dress in ballet costumes. She even sent me to the New York City Ballet Company to hire three ballerinas to perform.

"This is way too much pink," Olivia whispered in my ear. "It's like a pink unicorn threw up all over the place."

"Stop it." I laughed.

All of Mrs. Lake's guests started to arrive, and the competition between the mothers began. Fifteen little girls ran into the home, dressed in their finest and most expensive ballet costumes and shoes. Their hair was pulled up in a bun, and their makeup was exaggerated.

"Good God. I need a drink," Olivia said.

"We don't drink at our client's parties."

"She's not my client." Olivia walked away.

I went into the kitchen to make sure the catering staff was on top of everything. When I walked out, I froze, my heart racing, when I saw Charlie standing there.

"Marley?" His brows furrowed.

"Hey, Charlie. What are you doing here?"

"Uh, what are you doing here?" he asked.

"Mrs. Lake is my client."

"Client? What do you mean?"

"Ah, Charlie." Mrs. Lake walked over. "I see you've

met my event planner, Marley. Didn't she do an outstanding job?"

"Thanks, Mrs. Lake." I smiled.

"Event planner? I thought you were a barista?"

"Surprise." A grin crossed my lips. "I'm an event planner."

"You said you were a barista." His brows furrowed.

"No. I never said that. You just assumed. I was only helping Penelope and Olivia out. They own the place."

"I see."

"Charlie McBillionaire. Fancy seeing you here." Olivia walked over with a drink in her hand and stared at me.

"Hello, Olivia."

"Charlie, over here," Mr. Lake called over to him.

"We'll talk later," he said, walking away.

"How weird is that?" Olivia said, sipping her drink.

"That he's here?" I cocked my head.

"Yeah, and looking so damn fine, too." A grin crossed her lips.

"Give me that." I grabbed the drink from her hand and threw it down my throat.

As I ran around, ensuring the party was running smoothly, I couldn't help but steal small glances at Charlie as he and Chase stood and talked to Mr. Lake. He caught me, and when he winked, I quickly looked away. He walked over, lightly took hold of my arm, and leaned in so his lips were close to my ear.

"I'm leaving now. I'll see you tonight."

My brows furrowed. "What are you talking about?"

"I'm taking you to dinner. Olivia gave me your phone number and address and told me you don't have plans for tonight. So, you're having dinner with me."

"We had sex one time, Charlie. Why do you insist on making this weird?"

"Three times, Marley, and I like weird." The corners of his mouth curved upward. "I'll pick you up at seven." He walked away.

"Wait!" I shouted.

"I'll see you at seven." He kept walking.

"What the hell did you do?" I walked over to Olivia, who was eating a piece of cake, and grabbed her arm.

"This cake is so good. And what are you talking about?"

"You gave Charlie our address and my phone number?" I asked, cocking my head.

"Oh, yeah. I did. You can thank me later." She grinned.

"I don't want to go out with him tonight, Olivia."

"Yes, you do, Marley. If anyone is making things weird here, it's you." She pointed her fork at me. "What's the big deal? Charlie McBillionaire wants to take you out. Go and have fun."

"Will you stop calling him that?"

"No." She tapped my nose.

Chapter Nine

CHARLIE

The only good thing about this day was getting Marley's phone number and address so I could take her out. The deal between my company and Derek Lake still hadn't been closed, but after faking my happiness at his daughter's party, I was sure it would only be a matter of time.

After showering and dressing, I dabbed on some cologne and headed down to where the car service was waiting for me since my driver, Mateo, didn't work weekends.

Marley's apartment was right around the block from mine. Taking the elevator up, I knocked on the door.

"Oh, hello." Penelope smiled. "Come on in."

"Hi, Penelope. Olivia." I nodded as I saw her sitting on the couch.

As I stood there waiting for Marley, Olivia walked over.

"How did you enjoy the birthday party today?" she asked.

"It was nice if you like a bunch of little girls running

around screaming at the top of their lungs. Kids aren't my scene."

"Right? Mine either. I still have a headache," Olivia said.

My breath hitched when Marley entered the living room, looking as beautiful as ever.

"Hi." I smiled, tucking my hand in my pants pocket.

"Hi. I'm ready to go."

I placed my hand on the small of her back as we left the apartment.

"Nice car." She smiled, climbing into the back seat.

"This isn't my regular car. My driver has the weekends off."

"You have a driver?" she asked.

"Yes. His name is Mateo, and he's a great man. He's worked for me for seven years. Have you ever eaten at Salvatore's?"

"I have. Olivia told you it's one of my favorite restaurants, didn't she?"

"No." I chuckled. "It also happens to be one of my favorites as well."

When the driver approached the restaurant, I opened the door, climbed out, and extended my hand.

"Thank you, Charlie." Marley's lips gave way to a beautiful smile.

"You're welcome."

I opened the door to the restaurant, and when Marley stepped inside, her brows furrowed.

"This place is always packed. Why are we the only ones here?"

"Charlie." Salvatore walked over and shook my hand. "It's good to see you, my boy."

"Hi, Salvatore. I'd like you to meet Marley. Marley, this is Salvatore."

"Hello, sweetheart. Come with me." He led us to a table.

"I still don't understand why we're the only people here," she said.

"I bought out the restaurant for the night." A smirk crossed my lips.

"Why? I didn't even know people could do that."

"Salvatore is a family friend. He and my father go way back. I've been coming here since I was a kid."

"I will be personally serving you tonight." Salvatore smiled. "What can I get you to drink?"

"How about a bottle of your best white wine." I smiled.

"Excellent choice, Charlie." He walked away.

Within moments, Salvatore returned with a bottle of white and a bread basket.

"Are you two ready to order?"

"I'll have the chicken scaloppine with lemon and butter." Marley smiled.

"I'll have the same. Do you like calamari?" I asked her.

"I do."

"We'll start with an order of calamari, Salvatore," I spoke, handing him the menu.

"Very good." He nodded.

"Why, Charlie?" Marley asked, grabbing a piece of garlic bread from the basket.

"Why, what?"

"Why do you insist on making things weird?"

"Marley, I really have no idea why you keep saying that. Why is it weird that I want to take you to dinner?"

She leaned closer to the table and whispered, "Because we had sex last night."

"And? I can't take a woman I had a one-night stand with to dinner?"

"No. It's called a one-night stand for a reason. We had sex, and now any interaction between us is over."

"If you really believed that, you wouldn't have agreed to come."

"You forced me." Her eyes narrowed.

I chuckled. "I didn't force you."

"Yes. Yes, you did." She chewed her bread. "You wouldn't take no for an answer and scurried away without letting me say no."

Salvatore walked over and set the calamari in the center of the table.

"Enjoy, you two." He smiled.

"Thank you, Salvatore. "Well, since you think I forced you to have dinner with me, tell me about Marley—" I narrowed my right eye.

"Monroe." She picked up some calamari and put them on her plate.

"Tell me about Marley Monroe, the event planner."

"No."

"Excuse me?" My brow arched. "Listen, Marley. I explored every inch of your body last night, buried my cock deep inside you three times, and gave you countless orgasms. I think you owe me some information about yourself."

"I can't believe you just said that!"

"Why? Did it turn you on? Are your panties getting wet?"

"Stop it, Charlie." She pointed her fork at me. "And you forget about my panties."

"Not possible." I slowly shook my head. "I've never met a woman named Marley before. What's behind the name?"

She stared at me momentarily, popping a piece of calamari in her mouth.

"My parents are obsessed with Bob Marley. If I were a boy, I would have been named Robert and called Bob. Thank God I wasn't. When I came out a girl, they thought Marley was good enough to stick their daughter with that name."

"I know it's popular for a dog's name." I smirked, sipping my wine.

"Same goes for Charlie, Charles. It is Charles, correct?"

"It is, but I prefer Charlie, never Charles. Anyway, your parents sound cool."

"Why would you say that?"

"Because they named you Marley." I smiled.

"Well, they're far from cool. So, you can get that idea of them out of your head."

When she talked about her parents, her tone changed from fun to serious. I suspected she had ill feelings toward them, and I wanted to know why.

"What's wrong with your parents?" I asked.

"Nothing." She looked down at her plate.

Salvatore walked over and set our food down in front of us.

"Enjoy." He grinned.

"Always do, Salvatore." I smiled. "Tell me about your parents, Marley."

"No. Tell me about yours."

"Fine. My parents died in a helicopter accident when I was fifteen years old. I was supposed to be on that helicopter but didn't go because I was in a gaming tournament. I ended up living with my alcoholic aunt and sleeping on her couch in a one-bedroom eight hundred-square-foot apartment until I was seventeen and went off to college."

"I'm sorry, Charlie."

"Don't be." I finished my wine and poured another glass.

"My parents divorced when I was eleven years old. I don't like to talk about it because it's embarrassing."

"People get divorced all the time. That's nothing to be embarrassed about," I said.

"It is when your mother was having an affair with your next-door neighbor."

"Oh, shit. Seriously?" I asked with surprise.

"Yeah. They had been carrying on for a long time. My father found out and was furious. He filed for divorce the day after he found out. I remember the screaming matches they would have about it. He moved out, and I never forgave my mother for destroying our family."

"I'm sorry. What happened with your mother and the neighbor?"

"They got married. But that isn't the real kicker."

"No?" I asked, taking a bite of my food.

"No." She breathed out a laugh. "My father sought comfort with the ex-wife, and they also got married."

"Wait a second. You're telling me that your mother had an affair with the neighbor, got divorced, married the neighbor, and then your father married the ex-wife of the neighbor?" My brow arched.

"Yep." She popped her lips.

"Damn." I shook my head. "Holidays must be awkward."

"Holidays are separate. Even though the four of them are all happily married to each other's exes, they all hate each other, and my step-siblings and I are caught in the middle."

"You have step-siblings?"

"I do. I have two stepbrothers, twins, who are twenty-four."

"And you are——" I asked.

"Twenty-seven. So, they were eight when their parents divorced."

"Are the three of you close?"

"Not really. Our parents had joint custody of us. So, when it was my week to stay with my dad, the twins stayed at my house with their dad. They had the right idea, though. They got into Stanford and high-tailed it across the country when they turned eighteen. They're in medical school now. I only see them on holidays, if and when they come home. I only high-tailed it out of Long Island with Penelope and Olivia."

"Ah, you're from Long Island?"

"Born and raised." She smiled.

Chapter Ten

MARLEY

"Okay. Enough talk about parents. Why event planning?" he asked.

"Well, I'm creative and organized and like solving problems. Plus, I like challenges. It's very challenging to organize and put on events for some of the elite families in New York City."

"Like Mrs. Lake?" He smirked.

"Yes." I smiled.

"I think you did an excellent job with their child's party. Is that all you do is children's parties?"

"God, no. I've done a few small weddings, anniversary parties, engagement parties, showers, and bachelorette parties."

"Did you go to college?"

"I graduated from NYU with a bachelor's in business administration because I needed the knowledge to run my own business. I didn't realize how hard event planning would be to get into here in New York."

"How do you mean?"

"New York is filled with the best of the best. Nobody wanted to take a chance on someone just starting out. They want trustworthy and well-established planners who come highly recommended. Penelope's father is wealthy, and she convinced him to let me organize her parents' big anniversary party. After that, some jobs started rolling in. I'm a small fish trying to make it to the top with the sharks. I have to save every penny I make because I could go two, three, or sometimes four months without work."

"How did you get the Lake's party?" He tipped the glass to his lips.

"The woman Mrs. Lake hired unexpectedly moved to California, leaving Mrs. Lake high and dry. She called around to find another event planner, and all the top dogs were already booked. Miguel was the one who gave her my number and told her to call me."

"Who's Miguel?"

"He owns the florist where I get all the flowers for my events. Mrs. Lake stopped in one day to get flowers for a friend who was in the hospital, and she was complaining to him about her previous planner. Being desperate, she called and hired my company."

"What is your business name?"

"Marley Monroe Events."

We finished dinner, and after sharing a delicious dessert, we climbed into the back of the car.

"I have an idea," he said, grabbing my hand. "How about we go back to my place and have some fun."

"Didn't we have enough fun last night?" A smirk crossed my lips.

"Do you really remember last night?" he asked. "After all, you did ask me this morning if we had sex."

"I might remember a thing or two, but most is fuzzy."

"Then let me refresh your memory." He let go of my hand and softly stroked my cheek.

"Okay." I smiled.

"Do you need to tell your friends? I'm sure they'll be worried about you."

"Nah. I'm sure they're stalking my location as we speak."

The moment we stepped into the elevator, Charlie pushed me up against the wall, held my arms above my head, and smashed his mouth into mine. Feeling his lips on mine felt magical, and instantly, my body began to remember how he made me feel last night. The door opened, and we stepped into the foyer. Our lips locked as he unzipped my dress while my fingers fumbled with his belt. Kicking off my heels, I unbuttoned his shirt and slid it off his shoulders while his tongue explored my neck. The intensity of what was happening already had me soaking wet. He placed his palm on my belly and slid his hand down my panties, his fingers reaching my slick spot.

"Fuck, Marley. I need you right now." He picked me up, and my legs wrapped around his waist.

He carried me to the bedroom and lay me on the bed. His lips traveled to my breasts and wrapped around my hardened peaks. Shit. My body trembled with pure plea-sure like never before. He made his way down south, teasing me with every flick of his tongue and dipping a finger inside me. The sensation of an orgasm had my heart racing. This wasn't normal. He wasn't normal. How the hell did this man know exactly what my body wanted from him? I let out a pleasurable moan as the riptide tore into me. Charlie stood up and grabbed a condom. Sitting up, I stared at the beautiful outline of his hard cock through the fabric of his boxer briefs. God, this man was so sexy.

"My turn." I grabbed the sides of his waistband and

slowly pulled down his underwear, setting his throbbing cock free. Swallowing hard, I looked up at him. "This was inside me?"

"Three times." He grinned, looking down at me.

"Let's give this big guy some attention first." I wrapped my mouth around the head, taking him in slowly until it reached the back of my throat.

"Fuck, Marley." His chest rumbled with excitement. "Oh, my God." His moans grew with intensity as his fingers tangled in my hair. "Stop." He held my face in his hands. "I need to put this on and fuck you senseless."

"By all means, get to it." I smiled, lying on my back.

He rolled on the condom and hovered over me, grabbing my arms and holding them tight above my head. With one thrust, he was inside me, and I was on my way to the fun town of Pleasureville. His thrusts were deep, intense, and rapid. The moans that escaped our lips were ones of ecstasy and fulfillment. I came. He came. And our bodies melted when he lowered his on mine. He let go of my wrists, and my arms wrapped around him, softly stroking his muscular back. Our breathing was rapid but slowly returning to their normal rate. Before rolling off, his lips pressed against the side of my neck.

"Damn." I smiled as he rolled on his back.

"Damn is right." His breath was bated as his hand lay across his heart.

When he climbed out of bed to toss the condom in the trashcan, I lay there for a moment, waiting for my trembling body to calm itself.

"You're still in bed?" he asked, walking back into the room.

"I was just about to get up and get dressed. We don't need to make things weird."

"Yeah. I agree. I'll walk you home," he said.

"I live around the block, Charlie. I can walk home myself."

"If my calculations are right, it's a seven-minute walk back to your place. You are not risking seven minutes of your life on the streets of New York City after midnight."

"Look at you being all protective." I smiled as I slipped on my dress. "But seriously, I can catch an Uber." I grabbed my phone and pulled up the app.

"Stop. I'm walking you home." He took my phone from my hand.

"If you insist." I grabbed my shoes and put them on.

Charlie pulled on a pair of sweatpants and a T-shirt. I couldn't help but stare at him as he sat on the edge of the bed and slipped on his Nike tennis shoes. Damn, even like that, he was sexy as hell.

He walked me to my apartment building. I reached up and kissed his cheek.

"Thanks for walking me home. I feel like such a teenager." I grinned.

"You're welcome." He chuckled. "Listen, Marley. I don't want you to get the wrong idea."

"About what?" My brows furrowed.

"You're a great woman, but I'm not looking for anything. I don't want you to get the wrong idea that there could be a possible relationship between us. We had a good time, but that's it."

"You're making this weird, Charlie. I'm not that girl. I'm not looking for anything or anyone. That's not how I operate. But thanks for putting it out there and easing my mind. I was worried you would stalk me now because you fell madly in love with me, and I couldn't return the favor."

His eyes narrowed at me momentarily. "You're cute, Marley Monroe."

"Ah, so are you, Charlie Stone." I grinned. "Good night."

"Good night." His lips softly brushed against mine.

I opened the door to my building and took the elevator up to my apartment. Something wasn't right. I felt weird.

"Why are you home?" Olivia jumped up from the couch.

"Why aren't you sleeping?" I asked, setting down my purse.

"It's still early for me. You know that."

"What's going on?" Penelope bolted up from the couch, yawning and rubbing her eyes.

"Our girl just walked through the door," Olivia said.

"Why? You went back to Charlie's, and we know what you did. Why didn't you stay?"

"I said I didn't want to make things weird, and he agreed." I walked to my bedroom, opened the dresser drawer, and pulled out my nightshirt.

"Are you okay?" Olivia asked.

"Yeah, Mar, you seem off."

"I'm fine." I smiled. "Just tired."

I always told my best friends everything, but tonight, I couldn't because I didn't know how I felt.

Chapter Eleven

ONE MONTH LATER

CHARLIE

I was sitting behind my desk, staring out the window, when my office door opened, and Chase walked in.

"Are you ready to play?" he asked.

"Yeah." I sighed, turning my chair around.

We walked over to the couch, turned on the TV, and tested one of our new games.

"Have you talked to Marley?" Chase asked.

"No. Why?"

"I don't know. I just thought you might have called her. It has been a month since your last date."

"It wasn't a date. It was dinner and sex. Nothing else."

"You bought out Salvatore's for an entire night. That classifies as a date. Besides, Lila wants the four of us to get together."

"Then tell Lila to call Marley and do lunch or something. Why do I need to be involved?"

"Did someone take their pissy mood pills this morning?"

"Shit. Did you see that glitch?" I asked.

"No. What glitch?"

"Exactly. You're too busy grilling me about Marley and not paying attention to the game. Focus, Chase. You know how I operate."

"I'm sure she's missing your charm," he said.

"I made it very clear that I wasn't looking for anything, and so did she. She's not missing anything."

"Women lie. I'm sure she said that because of what you said."

"Drop it, Chase, and I mean it," my authoritative voice spoke.

"Whatever, Charlie. It's your life."

"Damn right, it is."

I left my office and walked a couple of blocks to pick up a sandwich for lunch. I could have had my assistant pick it up, but I needed some fresh air. My phone dinged with a text, so I looked down at it and suddenly bumped into someone.

"Excuse—Marley?" Our eyes locked.

"Charlie."

"How are you?" I asked.

"I'm really good. How are you? Sorry about slamming into you. I was looking down at my phone."

"Please, don't apologize. I wasn't paying attention either," I said.

"Well, it was nice to see you again." She smiled.

As she began to walk away, I turned and lightly took hold of her arm. She stopped and looked at me.

"I'm sorry I haven't called. I've been really busy with work."

"Don't apologize. I never expected you to. I really have to go, or I'm going to be late. Enjoy the rest of your day." A smile crossed her lips.

"Thanks. You too."

I sighed as I placed my phone in my pocket and continued walking to the deli. I knew I'd eventually run into her at some point. It wasn't that I didn't want to call her after that night and see her again; I couldn't. I had my reasons, and they were too personal to share with anyone, especially Chase.

MARLEY

I couldn't get away from him fast enough. Of all the men I'd semi-dated and had sex with over the years, no one had left a mark on me like Charlie Stone had. It took me almost three weeks to forget about him, and just when I thought I had, I ran smack dab into him because I was distracted by my phone.

"Thanks, Universe." I looked up at the sky. "Thanks a hell of a lot for that. I know you think you're really funny. Do me a favor. Next time, if I collide with someone on the street, make sure it's not him. Can you do that? Pretty please with sugar on top. Ugh."

I stepped into the Manhattan Diner and saw my dad sitting at a table, holding the menu.

"Hey, Dad." I smiled, kissing his cheek before taking the seat across from him.

"Hi, sweetheart. It's been a while."

"I know. I've been really busy." I picked up my glass of water and took a sip.

"Another event to plan?" He smiled.

"Yes. How are you?"

"I'm good. You look like you've lost some weight. Are you okay?"

"Dad, I haven't lost any weight, and I'm good. Stop being silly."

A waitress walked over and asked if we were ready to order.

"I'll have the tuna melt with a side of French fries." I closed my menu.

"I'll have the same," my dad spoke. "So, Marley. I ran into your mother last week at the market."

"I'm sorry about that."

He sighed and folded his hands on the table. "She said she hasn't seen you in months and barely speaks to you on the phone."

"I'm just a twenty-seven-year-old woman living her best life as an event planner and very busy."

"That may be, but you can't forget about your parents."

"I haven't forgotten about you or Mom. You're being dramatic, Dad."

"What's been going on with you? Is there a special man you're keeping a secret in your life?"

"Nope. No special man." I smiled as our waitress walked over and set our food down.

"Maybe a special woman?" He picked up his tuna melt.

"DAD!" I cocked my head.

"What? How am I supposed to know when you don't tell me anything about your life? All I want is for my baby girl to find someone special, get married, and have children. I'm ready to be a grandpa, you know."

I breathed out a laugh. "Well, you can forget about that. You and Mom both showed me how destructive love can be, and I'm not signing up for any of that shit. No way." I bit into my sandwich.

"Marley, I know it was rough for you growing up and being shuffled back and forth every other week between houses. What did you want me to do? Stay with your mother and pretend she wasn't fucking, Peter?"

"No. Of course not."

"I did the best I could with you under the circumstances. You need to let what happened between your mother and me go. It wasn't entirely your mother's fault, Marley. I let my work consume me to provide a better life for both of you than I had growing up. I wasn't around as much as I should have been."

"That's no excuse to run into the arms of our next-door neighbor, Dad. Besides, you hate her too for what she did."

"I've come to realize that your mother and I were meant to be together for a season in order for you to be born. The world is much better with you in it, sweetheart." He smiled.

"I see Miranda's been in your ear."

"My wife and I are very much in love. Everything happens for a reason. One day, you'll understand that."

After we finished lunch, I kissed my dad goodbye and headed to Love At First Sip.

"Look what the cat dragged in." Olivia grinned. "Shouldn't you be out shopping for décor?" She hooked her arm around me as I stepped behind the counter.

"What's wrong? You have that look," Penelope said.

"I ran into Charlie."

"What was his piss poor excuse for not calling you in over a month?" Olivia's brow arched.

"Same old, same old. He's been super busy with work." I rolled my eyes.

"No excuse." Olivia's grip around me tightened.

"It's not like I care."

"Yeah, you do." A smirk crossed Penelope's lips.

"No. I don't." I grabbed a cup and handed it to her. "Make me a latte with almond milk."

"I hate to break this party up, but I have to run to the store," Olivia said, grabbing her purse.

"For?" I asked.

"Tampons. I started my period and only had one tampon in my purse."

My phone rang, and when I pulled it from my purse, I saw my gynecological office was calling.

"Hello."

"Is this Marley?"

"Yes. This is she."

"Marley, it's Margo from Dr. Gregario's office. Our records indicate that you never showed up for your appointment last month. We were reaching out to see if you wanted to schedule something.

"What do you mean? I have an appointment next week for my Depo shot. I have it on my calendar."

"No. That appointment was last month, and you didn't show."

"I'm sorry, but you're mistaken. It's next week."

"Perhaps you accidentally put it in the wrong month. I've done that myself. Let me see what we have available next week. We had a cancellation for next Tuesday at noon. May I put you in?"

"Yeah. I guess. Thanks for calling, Margo. I'll be there."

"Girl, you're turning fifty shades of green. What happened?" Olivia asked.

I scrolled back through my calendar until I reached the last time I had the shot.

"Fuck! I fucked up." I stared at my friends.

"Fucked up, how?" Penelope asked.

"I put my Depo shot appointment in the wrong month.

I totally missed it last month. Oh my God! I missed a full month of birth control!" I panicked.

"Relax," Olivia said. "You haven't had unprotected sex or sex at all since Charlie. You specifically said you were back on your sex hiatus."

"Yeah, Mar. You're fine." Penelope smiled.

"I know I am. It's just how could I have been so stupid?"

"It happens to the best of us. Forget about it. You'll go next week, get your shot, and be back in the land of the protected," Olivia said.

Chapter Twelve

MARLEY

"Marley?" The nurse called my name as I sat in the waiting room.

Grabbing my purse, I stood from my chair and followed her into a room.

"I see you missed your Depo shot last month," she said.

"Yeah. I put my appointment in the wrong month on my phone. I don't understand why someone didn't call me to confirm my appointment. Your office always calls."

"A new receptionist started last month and obviously didn't confirm all the appointments. You're not the only one who didn't get a confirmation call."

"Your periods have ceased since being on the shots, correct?"

"Yes. I haven't had one since I started them."

"Okay. Dr. Gregario will be in shortly." She smiled.

I sat on the table, swinging my legs back and forth and looking at the pictures on the wall of the growing stages of a baby.

"Marley." Dr. Gregario grinned, stepping inside. "How are you?"

"I'm good, Dr. Gregario." I smiled.

"Let's see." He sat on the stool and typed away at the computer sitting on the counter. "Oh boy. You missed your Depo shot last month. Have you been sexually active?"

"Yes."

"Any unprotected sex?"

"Nope."

"Okay. Good. But since you missed your shot last month, we do need to draw your blood and run a quick pregnancy test just to be sure there isn't a little peanut growing inside you."

"I can assure you, Dr. Gregario, that there is no little peanut inside me."

"I believe you, but we still have to check. Our lab only takes about ten minutes to run the test. I'll send my nurse in to draw your blood, and I'll be back in with your shot."

He walked out of the room. I hopped off the table, grabbed my phone from my purse, and checked my emails. After the nurse drew my blood, I waited.

The door opened, and Dr. Gregario stepped inside empty-handed. He walked over to the table and gripped my hand, which I thought was odd.

"Marley, you're pregnant."

My heart started racing faster than the speed of light, and dizziness swept over me.

"Excuse me? That's impossible. Oh my God. I'm going to pass out." I quickly lay down on the table.

"Slow, deep breaths, Marley. You said you didn't have unprotected sex."

"I didn't!"

"Either you did, or the condom broke. You did skip

your shot last month. Are you okay?" he asked as I started hyperventilating.

"No, I'm not okay!" I shouted. "Your test is wrong. Run it again."

"I'm afraid the test is right. Perhaps you don't remember having unprotected sex."

"No. No. No." I placed my hand on my forehead. "I DID NOT HAVE UNPROTECTED SEX!"

"Breathe, Marley. This isn't good for you or the baby."

I stared at him when he said that, and suddenly, tears poured from my eyes.

"It'll be okay." He patted my hand. "You have options. You realize that, right?"

I slowly nodded as he helped me sit up.

"That a girl." He squeezed my hand. "You're around five weeks. So, I'll tell the girls to squeeze you in for next week, and we'll officially start your OB care." He smiled. "That's if you plan on carrying the baby."

"What do you mean, Dr. Gregario?" I started to cry again. "I could never have an abortion, no matter how bad things are."

"Phew, I'm so happy to hear you say that. I'll see you next week, Marley."

I walked out of the room, scheduled next week's appointment, and walked down the street, all dazed and confused. How could this have happened? I hailed a cab and took it back to my apartment. I was grateful Penelope and Olivia were still at the café because I needed time alone to think and clear my head. The baby had to be Charlie's because of the timeline.

"Fuck. Fuck. Fuck." I smacked the sides of my head with my hands.

Although it was only four o'clock, I took a bath, changed into my pajamas, and ordered an extra-large pizza. When the pizza arrived, I took a couple of pieces over to the couch and turned on The Notebook, my go-to movie when I was upset.

The door opened, and the girls walked in, laughing about something. They stopped when they saw me on the couch.

"She's eating pizza and watching The Notebook," Penelope whispered. "This isn't good."

"Mar?" Olivia walked over, sat next to me, and placed her hand on my arm. "What's wrong?"

"Yeah, sweetie. Did something happen?" Penelope took a seat on the other side of me.

"No. I'm just pregnant," I blurted out.

"WHAT!" They both shouted at the same time.

"You're kidding, right? Tell us you're kidding around," Olivia said.

"I wish I were." Tears streamed down my face.

"Oh, Marley." Penelope hugged me.

"Who's the baby daddy?" Olivia asked.

"I don't want to talk about it," I cried.

Her jaw dropped. "No way. Is it McBillionaire's? You have a baby McBillionaire inside you?"

"Olivia, can you not?" Penelope said. "How far along are you?"

"Five weeks. My life is over. A kid never even crossed my mind. I can't be a mom. I don't know how to be a mom. I don't know shit about taking care of a kid. I can barely take care of myself."

"You have options," Olivia said.

"OLIVIA!" Penelope shouted. "I can't believe you."

"I wasn't referring to an abortion. There are a lot of couples out there who can't have kids."

"She's not giving up her baby," Penelope said. "Right, Marley? You wouldn't do that, would you?"

"I don't know." I cried, covering my face with my hands. "What kind of life could I give this kid?"

"An amazing one with all that money Daddy McBillionaire is going to have to pay in child support," Olivia spoke.

"How am I going to tell him? He couldn't even be bothered to call me in over a month."

"You go over to his place and say, 'Charlie, I'm pregnant. What are you going to do about it?'" Olivia said.

"No, she is not," Penelope said. "You're going to calmly tell him in a nice way."

"He doesn't like kids. Hell, I'm not sure I even do." I threw my hands up in the air.

"She's right. You should have seen him at the Lake's birthday party. A little girl walked up to him, tugged on his pant leg, and he shooed her away, telling her that little hands are not to touch his expensive designer pants," Olivia said.

"Oh shit! How the hell am I going to tell my parents?"

"You're twenty-seven years old. Your parents are the least of your worries," Olivia sighed.

"We're here for you." Penelope rubbed my back. "Right, Olivia?" She cocked her head.

"You know it, babe. Everyone else in the world may turn their backs on you, but we won't and never will."

"I need to find out how this happened. It must have happened the night we were both drunk—the night of his housewarming party."

"You don't remember if he used a condom?"

"I don't really remember having sex with him! But yet, he said we did three times that night."

"All I can say is that you have to tell him tomorrow and get some answers. You can't put it off. Like my mom always says, putting off the inevitable makes it ten times worse," Penelope said.

"I just want to go to bed. Maybe I'm trapped in a horrible nightmare, and everything will be okay when I wake up in the morning."

"You'll still be trapped in that nightmare for the next eighteen-plus years," Olivia said.

"OLIVIA!" Penelope scowled.

"Sorry. Sorry. Come on." She grabbed my arm and pulled me up from the couch. "Slumber party in your bed tonight."

∽

The Next Day

CHARLIE

It was eight o'clock when I stepped off the elevator and into the foyer. Setting my briefcase down, I changed out of my suit and poured a glass of scotch. After the day I had, I needed it. I was about to head to the kitchen for something to eat when my penthouse phone rang.

"What's up, George?" I asked the doorman.

"There's a Marley Monroe here to see you, sir."

I furrowed my brows momentarily. Why would she be here?

"Send her up."

I stood in front of the elevator, waiting for it to come up. When the doors opened, she flew out and into the living room without so much as a hi.

"Marley, what are you doing here?"

"I have one question for you, and you better tell me the truth."

"Okay. What's your question?"

"Did you use a condom on the night we had sex after your housewarming party?"

My heart started racing with fear, and I suddenly broke into a pool of sweat.

"Why are you asking me that?"

"Don't answer a question with a question, Charlie. You said we had sex three times that night. Did you use a condom all three times?"

Fuck. Why was she asking me this?

I inhaled a deep breath as I finished my scotch, walked over to the bar, and poured another.

"You want the truth?" I asked her.

"Yes, I want the truth!"

"I know we used one. As for the other two times, I'm not sure."

"You're not sure!" she shouted.

"What is going on here, Marley?" I asked nervously as I sweated bullets.

"I'm pregnant, Charlie, and you're the father."

"How is that possible? Aren't you on birth control?" My voice raised.

"I put my shot appointment in the wrong month on my calendar. I missed it last month."

"A shot? You're not on the pill? Something you could take every single day instead of having to remember to get a shot every three months or however the fuck it works?" I shouted.

"I didn't want to have to remember to take a pill every day!" she shouted back. "The shot is easier."

"Obviously, not for you!"

"Stop yelling at me!" she shouted.

I put both my hands up and tried to calm the fuck down.

"Okay, I'm sorry. But you really caught me off guard," I said.

"You? You're caught off guard? How the hell do you think I feel?"

"Well, you have options. There's always an—"

She held up her finger. "Say it, and your balls will be hurting for weeks. I am not having an abortion."

"Okay, Marley. What the hell do you want me to do? Because if you're asking me to be a father to that kid, the answer is no. I don't want kids. Fuck," I rubbed the back of my neck, "I can't even commit to a relationship with a woman, let alone be a father. No. Absolutely the fuck not. I'm sorry, but if that's what you're looking for, it won't happen."

She stood there and stared at me as tears streamed down her face.

"This—this is all your fault! You and those little sperms of yours! Do you think I want this any more than you do?"

"You're a strong woman, Marley. You'll figure it out. If you keep the baby, I'll support you financially. But a kid doesn't fit into my lifestyle."

"Really, Charlie?" She cocked her head. "You're basically a kid yourself, sitting around playing video games all day!"

"It's my job!" I shouted. "My business. A business that makes me a hell of a lot of money! A company I started and grew to the top. How many thirty-year-old men can say that?"

"Ladies and gentlemen. The award for the biggest douchebag in the world goes to Charlie Stone." She began clapping.

"Like I said. You have options. If you choose not to explore those options, that's on you." I pointed at her.

"Enjoy the rest of your life, asshole!" She stormed past me and to the elevator. "By the way. Everything that happened between us never did. We never met, slept together, nothing. Keep walking when and if you see me on the street because I know I will. You're nothing but a stranger. And do yourself a favor. Go get a vasectomy if you don't want kids."

"I most likely will now," I said.

She shook her head as she stepped into the elevator. The doors shut, and I stood there trying to catch my breath.

Chapter Thirteen

MARLEY

I stepped into my apartment, sobbing. Olivia ran over and hooked her arm around me.

"I assume it didn't go well with Charlie." She led me to my bedroom.

"He doesn't want to take responsibility," I cried. "A kid doesn't fit into his lifestyle."

"He said that?"

"Yep, and other hurtful things. He kept telling me I have options."

"Did you tell him you're not getting an abortion?"

"Yep. He said he'd help financially, and that's it. What am I going to do, Olivia? I can't raise this kid on my own."

We heard the apartment door open.

"We're in Marley's room," Olivia shouted.

"Hey, what happened?" Penelope sat on the bed next to us.

"McBillionaire doesn't want the kid. He said he'd help her financially, and that's it," Olivia told her.

"Ugh, Mar. I'm sorry." Penelope hugged me. "All this stress isn't good for you or the baby."

"She's worried about raising the baby alone," Olivia spoke.

"You're not alone. We already told you that we're helping you. Plus, you have your parents," Penelope said.

"That's comforting." I blew my nose into a tissue.

"All I can say is what's done is done." Olivia stood up, walked over to the dresser, and pulled out one of my nightshirts. "Now, you're going to stop feeling sorry for yourself and start taking care of yourself. Fuck Charlie McBillionaire."

"Yeah," Penelope said. "Fuck him. He said he'll support you financially, and that's all that matters."

"I'm not taking a dime from him. I never want to see him again. Besides, I told him we're now strangers who never met, and if he sees me on the streets, keep walking."

"Now, you're just being stubborn," Olivia said. "There's no way we're letting you not take his money."

"So he never used a condom that night?" Penelope asked.

"He said he knows for sure we used one. As for the two other times, he wasn't sure."

"It's obvious now he didn't," Olivia said. "Fuck him. We got this. Right, Penelope?"

"That's right. We've always stuck together through the good and the bad. You're not alone, Marley."

"I know. Thanks, you two. I love you both so much."

"We love you too, girl." Olivia and Penelope hugged me tight.

CHARLIE

"Good—wow, you look like shit," Chase said, walking into my office.

"I feel like it too." I sighed.

"Are you sick or something?" He took the seat across from my desk.

"Yeah. I'm sick to my stomach, but not in an illness type of way."

"What are you talking about?" His brows furrowed.

"Marley came by the penthouse last night. She's pregnant."

"Oh, shit, Charlie." Chase ran his hand down his face. "Are you sure it's yours?"

"Yeah. I'm sure. She's five weeks, which puts it at the time of my housewarming party."

"I guess you did have a reason to worry when you only found one condom. She's not on birth control?"

"Apparently, she gets these shots and missed one because she put her doctor's appointment in the wrong month on her calendar."

"Is she keeping it?"

"She said she is. I told her I want nothing to do with it and that I'd help her financially."

He sat there, narrowing his eyes. "That's a bastard thing to do."

"Yeah, well, I'm a bastard."

"No, you're not. I know why you're the way you are. I'm your best friend. Nobody knows you like I do. I think you'd make a great father."

"Knock it off, Chase."

"Nah. You're just in shock. Once it wears off, you'll adapt to the situation."

"No, I won't. Marley told me that we're strangers now

and never met. She told me to keep walking if I see her on the street because she'll do the same."

"I hear sadness in your voice. You like her, and don't try to deny it. You didn't call her for a month after the night you took her out because you started feeling something, and you ran. Don't forget that I was here when you ran into her on the street that day. I saw the look of despair on your face."

"You're crazy and don't know what the hell you're talking about." I raised my voice.

"I know exactly what I'm talking about, Charlie. But there's nothing I can say or do." He stood up from his seat. "I can't help someone who doesn't want to be helped. I'll talk to you later."

Turning my chair around, I stared out at the busy city. My entire world crashed down on me, leaving me gasping for air. I couldn't help the way I felt. Kids were never part of my life's plan. Commitment was something I couldn't do. I was committed to the one thing in life that I knew I could control: my company. Babies cause drama—a lot of drama—things I had no control over.

I turned my chair around and picked up my phone. Pulling up Marley's number, I sent her a text.

"Last night was a clusterfuck, and we both said things we shouldn't have. I'm sorry. I want to meet you somewhere and give you a check to deposit into your bank account. You're going to need it. Don't fight me on this, Marley. It's the least I can do."

"New phone. Who dis?"

I sighed and rolled my eyes.

"You know damn well who this is."

"I regret nothing I said last night. And everything I did say I meant. I don't want your money now or ever. Keep it and keep walking away. In fact, run as fast as you can. Apparently, it's what you're best at in life. Don't text me again!"

I threw my phone across my desk, walked over to the bar, and poured myself a scotch. I didn't give two shits if it was only ten o'clock in the morning.

Chapter Fourteen

ONE WEEK LATER

MARLEY

"There she is." Dr. Gregario smiled when he stepped into the room. "How are you feeling, Marley?"

"Not good. Morning sickness has hit me with a vengeance, Dr. Gregario. But it's not just in the morning. It's all damn day."

He chuckled. "Yeah, that can be brutal. It'll get better within the next couple of months or so. I see you brought two of my other patients with you." He smiled. "Hello, Penelope. Hello, Olivia."

"Hey, Dr. Gregario." They smiled.

"You're six weeks now, so I want to do a transvaginal ultrasound."

"Why?" I asked.

"I like to do them just to make sure everything looks okay and that the pregnancy is viable. Are you ready?"

"I guess." I looked at Penelope and Olivia, who were on each side of me, holding my hand.

"Okay. You'll feel a bit of pressure—no big deal. Just relax."

I stared at the screen but didn't know what I was looking at.

"Oh boy," Dr. Gregario said.

"It's a boy!" Olivia blurted out.

"No. It's way too early to see that." Dr. Gregario stared at the screen.

"Dr. Gregario, is everything okay?" I nervously asked.

"Everything is fine, Marley. See this?" He drew a circle around an area.

"Yes."

"This is your baby."

"Awe!" Both Olivia and Penelope whined.

"And see this?" He drew another circle, and suddenly, I felt sick.

"Yes." I swallowed hard.

"That is also your baby."

"TWINS!" I shouted.

"Oh, shit," Olivia spoke in a low voice while Penelope tightly squeezed my hand.

"Yes, Marley. You're pregnant with twins."

I lay on the table and began to hyperventilate.

"Slow, deep breaths, Marley." Dr. Gregario removed the transducer and clasped my shoulders. "Slow, deep breaths. Relax."

My breathing began to return to normal as I lay there and tried to process the fact that I was carrying twin babies.

"You good?" he asked.

I slowly nodded.

"Okay. Let's do this again, and you'll see your twin babies' heartbeats."

"I bet you'll be taking McBillionaire's money now," Olivia said as we left the doctor's office.

"OLIVIA!" Penelope snapped.

"Just saying."

"Thanks for coming with me, but I just need to be alone right now."

"I don't think that's a good idea," Penelope said.

"Yeah, Mar. You shouldn't be alone right now."

"I'll be fine." I held my hand up for a cab. "I'll see you two later." I hugged them.

"Where to, miss?" the cab driver asked.

"Central Park."

I spent the next four hours in Central Park, sitting on a bench and thinking as I placed my hand on my belly. Twins. I didn't even know twins ran in my family.

A woman pushing a double stroller took it upon herself to sit down next to me.

"Hi." She smiled. "I hope you don't mind. My husband is meeting me here at this spot."

"Hi. Not at all."

She reached inside the stroller and pulled out a baby. The other baby in the stroller started to cry.

"Twins?" I gulped.

"Yeah." She smiled. She reached in and placed a pacifier in the mouth of the child in the stroller. "You be a good boy while mommy feeds your brother."

She threw a blanket over her shoulder and began to breastfeed.

"You have your hands full," I said.

"Not really." Her lips gave way to a smile. "My husband is a huge help. I don't know what I would do if I didn't have him."

"That's great," I said. "There's nothing like the support from the father of your children."

A few moments later, a man walked over to where we sat, kissed the woman on the cheek, reached into the stroller, and took the baby out.

"There's my big boy. Daddy missed you." He held him up.

I couldn't sit there anymore, so I told the woman it was nice to meet her and walked away. As I was walking the path to exit the park, I stopped. Rage filled my body.

"Oh, hell no. You aren't getting away with it, Charlie Stone."

I hailed a cab back to my apartment. Walking through the door, Penelope and Olivia jumped up from the couch.

"Are you okay? What did you do in Central Park all that time?" Penelope asked.

"Thinking. A lot of thinking." I went to my bedroom and grabbed my large suitcase from the corner.

"What are you doing?" Olivia asked.

"Making sure Charlie Stone steps up to the plate."

"You're scaring me, Mar," Penelope said.

"Girl, what are you on?" Olivia asked.

"Nothing. He impregnated me, and he's not taking the easy way out. I'm moving in with him."

Penelope gasped. "You just can't do that."

"You want to watch me. He's going to be a father to these babies he put inside me."

"That's my girl!" Olivia grinned.

"Let's be real. There's barely enough room for the three of us here, let alone two children," I said, throwing clothes into my suitcase. "I can't afford to move right now, and he has that monstrous penthouse." I went into the bathroom to collect my things.

"I don't think that's a good idea," Penelope said. "Just calm down. We'll figure things out."

"I already did." I shut my suitcase and zipped it. "I'll get the rest of my things later this week."

"Ha. Charlie McBillionaire isn't going to know what

hit him when hurricane Marley blows through." Olivia laughed, clapping her hands.

CHARLIE

I had stopped on the way home and got a carry-out from the Thai place around the corner. Just as I sat down to eat, my penthouse phone rang. Walking over, I answered it.

"Mr. Stone, there's a Marley Monroe here to see you."

I swallowed hard. Maybe she changed her mind about the money.

"Send her up."

I walked over to the elevator, and when the doors opened, she stepped into the foyer, pulling a large suitcase behind her.

"Um, what's going on?" I asked.

"I'll tell you what's going on?" she said, placing her hand over her mouth. "What is that smell?"

"Thai food. I was just about to sit down and eat."

She let go of her suitcase and ran to the bathroom down the hall. I followed and stood in the doorway, leaning against the door with my arms folded.

"What's wrong with you? Are you sick or something?"

"I'm pregnant, you idiot! All-day sickness. The smell of that Thai food sent me over the edge." She continued to vomit.

"What are you doing here, Marley? And why do you have a suitcase with you?"

She wiped her mouth with a tissue and stood up. "I'm moving in." She pushed past me.

"Excuse me? I don't think so."

She stopped, turned around, and jammed her finger into my chest.

"Oh, yes, I am. Guess what, Charlie? I had my first ultrasound today."

"Okay? And?"

"It's twins. TWINS! Not one baby, but TWO! You did this to me." She kept jamming her finger into me. "And now, you're taking on the responsibility as a father, whether you like it or not."

I began to sweat. Twins? This couldn't be happening.

"I can't raise two babies alone, and my apartment is too small to put two children in there. But the twin's father has this monstrous penthouse that would be perfect for all of their needs."

I ran my hands down my face and walked over to the couch.

"Are you done ranting and raving like a lunatic?" I looked up at her.

"Maybe?" She cocked her head and folded her arms. "I guess it depends on the next words that come out of your mouth."

Honestly, I was too scared to say anything.

"Marley, listen," I calmly spoke. "You just can't barge in here and say you're moving in."

"The hell I can't. If you want me gone, you'll have to call the cops."

"Fine." I pulled my phone from my pocket and began to dial 9-1-1, then stopped and threw it on the couch. "We need to discuss this like the adults we are. Come and sit down."

"You go eat your dinner first, and I'll sit out on the terrace so I don't throw up again."

"I no longer have an appetite." I stood up, walked over to the kitchen table, and tossed the Thai food. Taking the bag from the trash can, I tied it shut, walked over to the trash shoot, and threw it down to quickly get the smell out of the house.

"You didn't have to do that," she said.

"The last thing I need is you throwing up all over the place." A smirk crossed my lips. "I do need some fresh air, so you go sit out on the terrace, and I'll join you in a minute."

"Okay."

I walked over to the bar, poured myself a glass of scotch, and took it out on the terrace.

"Twins?" I asked, sitting down in the chair next to her.

"Yep." She popped her lips. "Charlie, I know you have a lot of issues, and so do I."

"I don't have any issues, Marley. It's just I have a life plan, and it doesn't include babies or drama."

"No, you have issues." She glanced at me. "But who the hell doesn't? I can't live in that apartment with two babies. It's not fair to Penelope and Olivia."

"But you think it's fair to me?" I arched my brow.

"I'm going to ignore that because you're simply an idiot and a child who isn't emotionally developed yet."

"And you are?" I breathed out a laugh.

Chapter Fifteen

MARLEY

"Women are more emotionally intelligent than men are. I'll reach my full emotional maturity when I reach the age of thirty-two. You, on the other hand, won't reach it until years later."

"You are full of shit." He laughed.

"Look it up. I learned about it in college. I always told myself that when I turned thirty-two, I'd be able to forgive my mother."

"So, we're just two emotionally immature adults with twins on the way?"

"Yep."

"And how is that fair to the kids?" I asked.

"Maybe you should have thought about that before not using a condom the second and third time." My brow arched. "One time just wasn't enough for you?" I narrowed my eyes.

He tipped the glass to his lips. "You initiated it the second time, from what I can remember. I guess we couldn't help ourselves."

"I guess not." I sighed.

"You really think you're moving in?" he asked.

"I don't think. I know. Please point me to the guestroom. I'm exhausted."

"Here's the thing. I don't have any beds in the other guestrooms. They're empty."

"Who has a penthouse this large and doesn't have an extra bed?" I furrowed my brows.

"I haven't gotten around to furnishing the other rooms."

"Okay." I inhaled a breath and stood up from my chair.

Stepping back into the penthouse, I grabbed my suitcase and wheeled it to his bedroom. Charlie walked in as I was in the bathroom, changing into my nightshirt and cleansing my face.

"What do you think you're doing?"

"Getting ready for bed." I turned and walked out of the bathroom and into the bedroom.

Walking over to the side of the bed that he didn't sleep on, I pulled back the sheets.

"Hold on a second. You're sleeping in here?"

"Yep. You really wouldn't let the pregnant mother of your twin babies sleep on a couch, would you?" I climbed in, set my phone on the nightstand, and pulled the sheets up. "It's not my fault you don't have an extra bed."

"Fine. Well, guess what? I'm sleeping in the bed as well. This is my bed."

"Never said it wasn't. You stay on your side, and I'll stay on mine," I said.

He stripped out of his clothes, and my eyes diverted to his sexy-as-sin body. Even though I wasn't a fan of his, I would let him take advantage of me.

"Goodnight, Marley." He rolled on his side, his back to mine.

"Night, Charlie. Sweet dreams."

"More like a nightmare." I heard him mumble under his breath, and I silently smiled.

I would make this as miserable for him as it was for me.

My eyes flew open, and I quickly sat up, covering my mouth with my hand. I jumped out of bed and ran into the bathroom. As I was hanging over the toilet, feeling as if my insides were coming up through my throat, Charlie walked in and started the shower.

"Morning. Can I say something?" he asked.

"What?"

"If you're going to be throwing up, please use the other bathroom."

I couldn't believe the nerve of this man. "How about I just don't get out of bed at all and throw up on you."

"Really, Marley?" He took down his underwear and stepped into the shower.

I was done vomiting but pretended I wasn't as I stole small glances at his cock that got me in this position to begin with. God, I was horny.

I wiped my mouth with a tissue and climbed back into bed. As I lay there, I heard the shower turn off. With a towel ·wrapped around his waist, Charlie entered the bedroom and removed one of his many suits from the closet.

"Why does a gamer wear a suit to the office?" I asked.

"I'm a CEO and have an important meeting today."

"But you're also a gamer. Shouldn't you dress like one?"

"Shouldn't you go back to sleep?" He walked past me.

I grabbed my phone from the nightstand and noticed a text message in our girl's group chat.

Olivia: "How did McBillionaire take it?"

Penelope: Come on, Mar. We're dying over here."

"I'll stop by the coffee shop later and tell you."

"Oh God." I placed my hand over my mouth and jumped up from the bed.

"Other bathroom!" I heard Charlie shout.

I ran into the other bathroom and barely made it. Hanging my head in the toilet, I wanted to die.

"I'm leaving now. I suppose you'll still be here when I get home?" Charlie asked from the doorway.

"Yep," I said.

I heard him sigh and walk away.

Climbing back into bed, I'd finally drifted off to sleep when I heard talking in the hallway.

"Oh, my God!" I heard a voice shout.

I quickly sat up and stared at the older woman with blonde hair pulled back into a bun.

"Who are you?" I asked.

"Who are you?" she asked back.

"I'm Marley."

"I'm Greta, Mr. Stone's housekeeper."

"Ah, I didn't know he had a housekeeper." I brought my knees up to my chest.

"He has two. Sylvia and I come in once a week and clean."

"Oh. Well, then, I guess we'll get to know each other. As I said, I'm Marley, and I'm pregnant with twins. Charlie is the baby daddy."

"Excuse me?" Her brow arched.

"I know." I sighed, climbing out of bed. "I'm just as shocked as you are. I'll get out of your way so you can make the bed."

"Take your time. I can start somewhere else," she said.

I dressed quickly, grabbed my purse, and headed toward the elevator.

"It was nice to meet both of you." I smiled. "I'll see you next week."

CHARLIE

"I think the meeting went great." Chase smiled.

"Yeah. I'm confident Danbury will do business with us," I said, climbing into the back of the sedan.

"We haven't had a chance to talk yet because of the meeting, but you seem off today—more off than usual since you found out Marley is pregnant."

"She showed up at my penthouse last night with her suitcase in tow."

"What?" Chase laughed.

"She said she's moving in. She found out she's pregnant with twins."

"What?" He laughed harder. "You're not serious?"

"Do I look like I'm kidding?"

"Where is she sleeping? You don't have any other beds in that place."

I sat there and arched my brow at him.

"Stop it!" He laughed. "You're letting her sleep in your bed?"

"Like I have a choice."

"Are you sleeping in it too?"

"Damn right, I am. It's my bed."

"I hope you're getting some action, at least." He chuckled.

"Knock it off."

"Twins. Wow. I can't believe it. Do you want my advice?"

"No."

"Too bad. You're getting it anyway. Make peace with Marley and the fact that you're going to be a father."

"I don't want to talk about this, Chase. You know where I stand."

"Yeah, I do. And I can see it so clearly. You're standing on the outside of your life, Charlie. Why don't you take a step inside and see how great it can be?"

"I have a great life."

"You think you do. That's your perception. But to us, the outside world, all we see is a man who lives for his games and his company, making billions every year with nobody to share it with. I'm going to ask you something, and I want the honest to God's truth from you. Have you had sex with anyone since Marley?"

"That is none of your business." I glared at him.

"Ha! I knew it. It's always been my business, Charlie. You always tell me about the women you fuck. And I got to thinking the other day that you haven't mentioned a word about sex since Marley."

"I've been busy with the launch. I haven't had the opportunity to find someone and get some action."

"Your hand must hurt." He smirked. "Because for as long as I've known you, you haven't gone one week without sex."

"Shut the fuck up." I shook my head.

My phone rang, and when I pulled it from my pocket, I saw Greta was calling.

"It's Greta." I looked at Chase. "Hello, Greta." I put it on speaker.

"Mr. Stone, Sylvia and I wanted to let you know that we're finished cleaning the penthouse."

"Okay. Thank you. You never call me when you're done." My brows furrowed.

"We met your baby mama, Marley. She seems very nice. But now that another person is living in the penthouse, it creates more work for us. We're going to have to up our rates."

Chase busted out into laughter.

"Fine, Greta. I understand."

"Okay, Mr. Stone. I just wanted to let you know. Goodbye."

"Just wait until the babies are born." Chase laughed. "She's going to triple her rate."

"Shut up." I sighed.

Chapter Sixteen

CHARLIE

I arrived home from work around eight o'clock, and all was quiet when I stepped off the elevator. Maybe she wasn't here. Perhaps she thought more about it and went back to her apartment.

"Marley?" I shouted.

"In your game room," I heard her yell.

Fuck.

I went into the bedroom to change my clothes before heading to the game room to see what she was up to. After pouring myself a scotch, I slid open the door and found her sitting crisscross on the couch, playing my newest game.

"What do you think you're doing?" I asked as she sat there in her nightshirt.

"Playing this game. You designed this?" She smiled.

"I did." I sat beside her. "You seem to be enjoying it."

"It's fun." She stared at the TV, her fingers tapping the buttons on the controller like a mad woman.

"I can't believe you just took that guy down. He's one of the hardest in the game." I laughed.

"Can I let you in on a little secret?" she said.

"Sure."

"I might be a little bit of a game nerd myself. I grew up playing video games in my room to drown out the noise of my parents fighting and to avoid the new step-daddy and step-mommy."

"I know you said you liked to play," I said.

She saved the game, picked up the remote, and turned off the TV.

"I played a lot when I wasn't hanging out with Penelope and Olivia. When did you start playing, and what led you to open your own company?"

"I was ten when I first started playing. When I was thirteen, I was getting bored because there was nothing out there that would hold my interest anymore. So, I figured I'd develop my own game—something I wanted to play."

"You developed your own video game when you were thirteen?" she asked with surprise.

"That's when I started teaching myself coding. I actually created the game when I was fourteen."

"You taught yourself how to code?"

"I did." I smiled. "I used the knowledge I learned and created what I wanted to play. After many playthroughs, ensuring there weren't any glitches and the game ran smoothly, I wanted to see if any of my friends in an online gaming forum were interested in playing. They said they'd test it out, and believe it or not, the game went viral overnight. Six months later, my parents received a call from Sony, asking if they could meet me. My parents and I met with them, and they offered me a huge sum of money to buy the rights to the game, plus royalties for three years.

They wanted to revamp it for their systems. I couldn't believe it. God, that was such a magical day, and one I'll never forget. My parents opened a bank account in my name and deposited the money and royalties. It was for my college fund. A year later, they were killed in that helicopter crash, and my life completely changed."

"Again, I'm sorry about your parents." She reached over and placed her hand on my shoulder.

"I appreciate it, Marley. My aunt barely made enough money to support herself and her drinking habit. She knew about the money Sony gave me and wanted to know where it was. I told her that Sony opened a special account for me, and I couldn't touch the funds until I turned twenty-one."

"And she believed you?"

"Yeah. Thank God my parents didn't give her too much information about it. She's not the sharpest tool in the shed. I'm not sure how she and my mom were even related. They were so opposite. Anyway, I knew I only had to live with her for a couple of years before I went off to college. The thing was, I didn't want to use that money for college because I knew I wanted to run my own company one day. I am a smart guy, believe it or not." I smiled. "I worked extra hard in school and received several scholarships to Yale. That's where I met Chase. He was my roommate freshman year and also loved gaming. It turned out we had spoken to each other in our gaming forum but had no idea who the other was."

"So, did you study gaming at Yale?" Her brows furrowed.

"No." I chuckled. "I studied business and finance. I knew I needed to learn everything I could if I wanted to run a successful company. While at Yale, Chase and I developed a couple of games and sold them around

campus for extra money. I told him that when we graduated, I was opening my own company, and I'd bring him
on as president, and he'd help me run it. We were twenty-
two when we graduated, and I opened the doors to Stone
Game Ventures a year later after securing more funds from
a private equity firm. Once I hit a billion dollars in the first
two years, I moved from a smaller space to where my office
is now."

"That's very impressive, Charlie. Your parents would
be so proud of you." A beautiful smile crossed her face.

"They were very proud of me. I just wish they were
here now to see my accomplishments. They were great
people and parents." I looked down at my glass. "I would
give it all away to have them back. Enough about them."

She climbed on my lap and took my face in her hands.
Instantly, my cock started getting hard.

"What are you doing?" I stared into her beautiful eyes.

"Taking a chance that you'll have sex with me. I'm
horny, Charlie, and it's too much work to have to go out
and find someone when your sexy ass is right here."

"I can help you with that." The corners of my mouth
curved upward.

"With what? Helping me find someone else?"

"Shut up, Marley." My mouth smashed into hers.

My fingers grabbed the ends of her nightshirt, and I
broke our kiss long enough to lift it over her head. My cock
grew harder as it ached to be inside her again. She pulled
my shirt off, and her fingers hooked into the waistband of
my sweatpants. I held onto her as I lifted myself up, and
she pulled them down while our lips stayed tangled. My
hands groped her breasts as my fingers grasped her hardened peaks. Soft moans escaped both of us as she rubbed
herself up and down my cock. The wetness that emerged
from her had me so hot that I couldn't wait.

"Ride me now," I commanded.

She lifted herself as I positioned my hard cock at her slick entrance, and she slowly inched down until I was buried deep inside her. I gasped at the warmth that enveloped me. Taking her breasts in my mouth, I paid extra attention to her nipples, listening carefully to every moan that escaped her lips. I could feel her getting ready to orgasm as she moved her hips back and forth. With a loud moan, she came, and a flood of warmth came with her. Standing up with her in my grip, I pushed her up against the wall, thrusting in and out as the intensity of an orgasm shot through me, and I exploded inside her.

I buried my face into her neck as my heart raced out of control. Closing my eyes, I took in her scent and held her tight.

"Fuck," she spoke breathlessly.

I lifted my head and stared into her eyes before they diverted to her lips and softly kissed her.

"You sure know how to make a woman's body feel good." A bright smile crossed her face.

"I do aim to please." I smirked, pulling out of her and carefully setting her down.

"You should be very proud of yourself." She walked over to where her nightshirt lay on the floor and slipped it on. "I'm heading to bed."

"Okay. I'll be heading there myself soon."

I pulled on my pants, grabbed my shirt, and went into the living room to pour a scotch. Taking it out to the terrace, I stood at the railing and stared into the night. My life was changing so fast, and I didn't know what to do or how to feel. One minute, I was this carefree bachelor living my best life, and the next, a woman, pregnant with my twins, moved into my penthouse.

After finishing my drink, I went into the bedroom and

stood at the edge of the bed, staring at Marley as she slept. Carefully climbing into bed, I pulled the sheet over me and placed my hands behind my head. Thoughts of what my life would be like in seven months scared the hell out of me. I was in no way ready to be a father, not now or ever.

Chapter Seventeen

MARLEY

"We had sex last night," I said, holding the warm cup between my hands.

"At least you don't have to worry about getting pregnant," Olivia said.

"So, things are good between you and Charlie?" Penelope asked.

"I wouldn't say that. It happened in the moment. There's a side to him he doesn't let out. I saw it last night."

"Probably because he's a fucked up billionaire," Olivia spoke.

"I don't think he ever got over his parents' deaths." I brought the cup to my lips.

"I don't think anyone ever really does," Penelope said. "I know your parents are still alive, but look at how you never got over their divorce."

"Shit." I sighed. "Do you think I have to tell them about the babies?"

"Really, Marley?" Penelope cocked her head.

"Just dodge them for the next seven months and then

pop over to their houses with one in each arm." Olivia grinned.

"Look at that line. We better get behind the counter and help," Penelope said.

"It's okay. I have an event to start working on."

"What event?" Olivia asked.

"Stella Bradshaw. One of my other clients' nannies referred me. She's throwing a surprise birthday party for her husband."

"The nanny of a client?" Olivia's brows furrowed.

"Yeah. I thought that was weird, too." I grabbed my purse and hooked it over my shoulder. "I'll talk to you girls later. Love you."

"We love you too!" They both shouted as I walked out of the café.

I knocked on the door of the Bradshaw home, and an older woman answered.

"You must be Marley." She smiled. "I'm Dora. Please come in."

"It's nice to meet you, Dora." I grinned.

"You can have a seat in the living room, and I'll let Stella know you're here."

"Thank you." I stepped into the living room and looked around.

"Marley. Hi, I'm Stella. It's nice to meet you finally." She walked into the room holding a newborn baby and extended her hand.

"Hi, Stella. The pleasure is mine. Aw, your baby is adorable." I smiled. "He looks brand new."

"He is." She laughed. "He's four weeks old. I have another son as well. Our nanny, Melissa, took him to the park."

"How old is he?"

"Not quite two years old yet."

Suddenly, a wave of nausea fell over me. Placing my hand on my belly, I prayed it would pass. It didn't, and I placed my hand over my mouth.

"Marley, are you okay?"

"Bathroom?"

"Down the hall. First door on the left."

I ran down the hall to the bathroom, shut the door, and vomited. I had never been so humiliated as I was at that moment. Who throws up at a client's home? Shit. This wasn't the impression I wanted to give. After I finished, I washed my hands and returned to the living room, where Stella was sitting on the couch with her baby.

"Are you okay? Do you need to reschedule?" she asked.

"I'm fine, just pregnant."

"Oh! Come sit down. Morning sickness sucks. I'm all too familiar with that. I had it with both of my children. Dora?" she shouted.

"Yes, Stella?" Dora walked into the room.

"Can you please make Marley some peppermint tea?"

"I sure will." She smiled.

"Peppermint tea helped me." She placed her hand on mine. "How far along are you?"

"Seven weeks."

"Wow. You're newly pregnant. Congratulations. You and your husband must be happy."

"This pregnancy happened by accident with too much alcohol involved. I'm not married." I bit down on my bottom lip. "And my babies' daddy is pissed off and doesn't want kids."

"I'm sorry. Did you say 'babies?'"

"I'm having twins."

"How wonderful." She grinned.

"Is it?" I cocked my head. "Is it really?"

"Well—I mean—okay, I'm sorry. And the father doesn't want kids?"

"Nope." I popped my lips. "But I'm not giving him a choice."

"How do you mean?" Stella asked.

"I was partially accepting the fact that I would be a single mother at first. But when I found out it was twins, I wasn't letting him off that easy. So, I moved into his penthouse."

"Well, at least he asked you to move in."

"No. He didn't ask me. I packed my things, showed up at his place, and told him I was moving in whether he liked it or not."

"Stop it!" She laughed. "You did not."

"Yes, I did. There's no way in hell I'm raising these babies by myself. He did this to me, and he will take responsibility."

"Oh my God. I love you!" She reached over and hugged me.

The front door opened, and Stella instantly panicked.

"What is my husband doing home?" she whispered as her eyes widened. "Just follow my lead."

"Hi, sweetheart." The handsome man walked into the room and kissed her cheek. "There's my big boy." He took his son from her.

"Miles, what are you doing home? It's the middle of the afternoon," Stella asked.

"I had a meeting not too far from here, and I figured I'd just come home and spend the rest of the day with you and the boys. Hi. I don't think we've met. I'm Miles."

"Hi, Miles. I'm Marley."

"Marley is my new friend," Stella said. "We met at the doctor's office when I went for my check-up. She's newly pregnant."

"Congratulations, Marley. So, Dr. Gregario, is your obstetrician as well?"

"Uh, yeah. He is. Love that guy." I grinned.

"You know, Miles. I wish you would have told me you were coming home because Marley and I were just on our way out to do some shopping."

"Oh. Well, it's okay. Go ahead and have fun. Where's Melissa?"

"She took Ben to the park."

"Then I'm going to take this one and relax." He smiled.

"Are you sure you don't mind if we go shopping?" Stella asked.

"No. Of course not." He kissed her lips. "I'll have Sean drive you, and I'll see you when you get home. I love you."

"I love you too." Stella smiled. "But we'll take a cab."

"Are you sure, sweetheart?"

"One hundred percent. Come on, Marley. Let's go shop."

We climbed into the back of the cab, and Stella let out a breath.

"So, tell me, Marley. Whose penthouse did you move into?" A smirk crossed her lips.

"His name is Charlie Stone."

She reached over and placed her hand on my arm. "Of Stone Game Ventures?"

"Yes. Do you know him?"

"I've met him once at a party my husband and I attended. My husband knows him well. He's a handsome man." A smile crossed her lips.

"He's broken. Shit. I'm broken. We're two broken people having two babies who will also most likely be broken."

"That is not true. Listen, Marley. Miles was way broken when we met."

I sat there in shock while she told me the story of how they met, their fake marriage, and everything that happened when she got pregnant.

"Even the most broken men can be fixed." She smiled. "Are you in love with him?"

"God, no. Well—no." I shook my head. "I can't be. I won't allow it."

"Okay." She patted my arm with a smirk on her face.

We ended up sitting on a bench in the park, talking about what she wanted for her husband's birthday party. I took notes. She was such a nice person, and I saw a friendship in the making.

Chapter Eighteen

ONE WEEK LATER

CHARLIE

Opening my eyes, I stared at her as she slept on her side. I still hadn't gotten used to the fact that she invaded my home the way she did. I'd never met anyone like her, and I knew the moment she sat down next to me in the Chicago airport I was screwed. And even more so the first time we'd slept together. I'd had sex with plenty of women in my life and had never felt the connection I did with Marley. I couldn't explain it, nor did I want to.

The loss I'd felt when my parents died affected me in a way that I never knew it possibly could. To lose two people whom I deeply loved at such a young age nearly destroyed me. I should have sought therapy at some point, but what was the point? I saw firsthand how life could change in a split second—how the world could turn upside down, leaving you in a lonely place, both physically and in your mind. Grief was the price you pay for love, and I'd shut myself off from ever putting myself in that situation and experiencing it again. I knew what I needed to do. It was best for Marley and the twins.

Her eyes flew open. She stared at me momentarily, placed her hand over her mouth, and flew out of bed. This was every morning. Climbing out of bed, I turned on the shower in the bathroom as she leaned over the toilet. She didn't listen to me when I asked her to use the other bathroom. She kept throwing up in the primary one every morning to spite me. Wiping her mouth with a tissue, she stood up and looked at me.

"God, I hate you." She shook her head and walked out of the bathroom.

I let out a soft chuckle as I stepped into the shower. When I finished, I wrapped a towel around my waist and went into the bedroom.

"You know what, Marley?"

"What, Charlie?"

"You say you hate me, but it takes two people to make a baby. We both screwed up. We were drunk, and I forgot to use condoms. But you, you were irresponsible with your birth control. So, this pregnancy is also on you."

"Shut up." She pulled the covers over her head, and I smiled. "Don't forget we're going to my dad's tonight to announce the pregnancy."

"Marley, I don't think—"

She threw the covers back and sat up. "I don't care what you think. I'm not going to my dad's house and doing this alone. Do you really want him to know that you want nothing to do with your children? Do you not care what people think of you?"

"Fine. I'll go."

"Thank you. We're going to dinner at my mom's house tomorrow night to tell her."

"Oh, come on, Marley."

"My dad is one thing, but if you think you're getting

out of going with me to my mother's house, you're sadly mistaken, buddy. You know the issues I have with her."

"Whatever," I growled as I walked out of the room.

I left for the office and didn't say goodbye to her. I was so angry that she was making me do this shit. Picking up my phone from my desk, I called my friend and realtor, Grant Roman."

"Charlie, my friend. Don't tell me you're looking to move already." He chuckled.

"No." I laughed. "Actually, I wanted to know if you're at the office. I need to stop by and talk to you about something."

"I am. Are you on your way now?"

"Yeah. I can be there in about fifteen minutes."

"Perfect. I'll see you then."

After Mateo dropped me off, I took the elevator to Grant's office.

"It's good to see you again, Charlie." We lightly hugged.

"Good to see you too, Grant."

"Have a seat. What can I do for you?"

"I need you to find an apartment for a woman I know."

"Okay. What type of apartment are you looking for?"

"At least a three-bedroom," I said.

"Buying or renting?"

"I'll buy it."

"May I ask who this woman is?"

I ran my hand down my face and sighed. "She's a woman I got pregnant. She's having twins."

"I'm not sure if I should congratulate you or not by the sound of your voice."

"You can save it. Anyway, she took it upon herself to move into my penthouse, and I can't have her there."

"Why?" His brows furrowed.

"It's complicated, Grant."

"Okay. I'll start looking right away. Does she know you're doing this?"

"No. I'll tell her tonight."

"Charlie, I—"

"Don't, Grant." I held up my hand. "I get enough lectures from Chase."

I had Mateo pick Marley up at the penthouse before picking me up from the office and heading to her father's house. This was the last thing I wanted to do, but I had no choice.

"Hey," I said, climbing into the backseat of the sedan.

"Hi." Marley smiled. "How was your day?"

"It was okay." I pulled out my phone and looked over some new emails.

"Aren't you going to ask about my day?" she asked.

"No."

"You're very rude. I really hope our kids don't inherit your rude genes."

"Enough, Marley," I snapped.

I glanced up at Mateo as he looked at me through the rearview mirror.

"Fine." She put her hand up.

Mateo pulled up to her father's building. Climbing out first, I extended my hand to her. She slapped it away and climbed out herself.

"Now, you want to be a gentleman. I don't think so," she huffed and walked into the building.

Shaking my head, I followed her to the elevator. I couldn't believe I was meeting her father and stepmother. We stepped inside and took it up to the thirteenth floor. Marley knocked on the door, and an older woman with blonde hair answered.

"Marley, it's good to see you." She hugged her. "Miranda, Charlie. Charlie, Miranda."

I smiled as I shook her hand.

"Is that my daughter?" I heard her father shout.

"Yeah, Dad," Marley said.

We stepped inside, and her father walked toward us, stopping dead in his tracks when he saw me.

"Oh, hello." He grinned, extending his hand. "I'm Jonathan Monroe."

"It's a pleasure, Mr. Monroe. I'm Charlie Stone."

"Trust me, Charlie. The pleasure is all mine. Hello, sweetheart." He kissed Marley's cheek. "Let's go into the living room, shall we? Charlie, you look like a scotch man."

"I am." A smile crossed my lips.

"Excellent. So am I." He walked over to the mini bar in the corner of the room. "I have to say, Marley, when you called and asked if you could come over, I was thrilled. Is it because you wanted to introduce your boyfriend to us?" He winked.

"Dad, Charlie isn't my boyfriend. He's the father of my babies."

Her father stood there frozen, holding a scotch in each hand.

"Excuse me?" he said.

"You're pregnant, Marley?" Miranda asked.

"Yep. Did you not hear the word 'babies' in my sentence?"

"Babies?" Marley's father cocked his head, handing me my glass of scotch.

"Yes, Dad. I'm having twins. I didn't know twins ran on Mom's side of the family," Marley said.

"Your grandmother was a twin."

"How did I not know that?" Her brows furrowed.

"Your grandmother's twin sister died at birth. It was

never talked about. I can't believe my baby is having two babies, and I'm going to be a grandfather. Have you told your mother yet?"

"No." Marley looked down. "We're telling her tomorrow. "Okay. Now that you know, we really have to go."

"Sweetheart, you just got here," her father said.

"I know, but I'm tired and not feeling well." She stood up and hugged him. "We'll meet for lunch or dinner soon. Come on, Charlie." She glanced at me.

She stared the whole ride home out the window and didn't say a word. I could tell she was upset, and maybe tonight wasn't a good time to tell her about Grant looking for an apartment for her. When we arrived home, I poured myself a scotch and took it into the bedroom, where Marley was changing into her nightshirt. I just needed to get it over with and tell her about Grant looking for an apartment for her.

"Marley, I need to talk to you about something."

"What is it?" She turned her head, and a small smile crossed her lips.

I stared into her eyes momentarily, and I couldn't do it. "I wanted to talk about your dad."

"What about him?"

"He seems like a great guy. I know I don't know him that well, but he didn't deserve what your mother did to him."

"I know." She sighed. "And he is a good man. Did you see the look on his face when I told him about the twins?" She grinned.

"Yeah." I chuckled. "His face lit up like a Christmas tree."

She went into the bathroom and began brushing her teeth. I followed and grabbed my toothbrush. As soon as I squirted some toothpaste on it, Marley ran to the toilet and started vomiting. Setting my toothbrush down, I walked over, grabbed her hair from her hands, and held it back until she finished.

"All better now?" I asked.

"Some. Thanks." A light smile framed her lips as she wiped her mouth with a tissue.

We pulled the covers back and climbed into bed.

"Night, Charlie," Marley said, turning the other way.

"Night, Marley," I said, placing my hands behind my head.

Glancing over at her, I thought about my parents and the one rule they always followed: No matter what happened during the day, we would never go to bed angry with each other. They made that promise to each other on their wedding day. And if they got into an argument, it was always resolved before bed. At first, I thought it was weird. I was a kid, and anything adult-related was strange to me back then. What they had was special. They were always laughing and dancing. My dad loved jazz music, and while my mother was cooking dinner, he'd put it on, take her hand, and they'd dance in the kitchen. Not a day went by when he'd tell her how special she was and how much he loved her. My life would have been so different if they were still alive, but their tragedy changed everything for me.

Chapter Nineteen

MARLEY

I heard the shower running. Sitting in bed, I placed one hand on my belly and the other over my mouth. The nausea was there, but the feeling and my stomach were different. Throwing back the cover, I climbed out of bed and stood in front of the full-length mirror, taking note of the sudden expansion that happened overnight.

"What are you doing?" Charlie walked into the bedroom with a towel wrapped around his waist.

"It's happening."

"What's happening?" He opened the dresser drawer and pulled out a clean pair of underwear.

"This." I pointed to my belly.

"I didn't see you run into the bathroom while I was in the shower. Did you finally listen to me and use the other one?"

"No. There's no need this morning." I smiled. "I'll go make you some coffee and me some peppermint tea."

I grabbed the bottle of prenatal vitamins from the kitchen counter and took one. While the water was brewing for the tea, I made Charlie a cup of coffee and set it on the island.

"Thanks for this." He grabbed the cup and held it up.

"You're welcome. Don't forget dinner tonight at my mom's house. We have to be in Long Island at six-thirty."

I heard him sigh.

"Oh, I'm sorry. Am I inconveniencing you? You know what, Charlie? Just forget it. You don't have to go. I'll tell my mom something came up, and I can't make it."

He stood there momentarily, narrowing his eyes at me with a smirk on his lips.

"What? Why are you looking at me like that?"

"You're trying to start an argument so you can blame me and use me as an excuse to cancel. I wasn't sighing at you. I sighed because of an email from a client with a problem." He held up his phone.

"No," I pointed at him, "you were sighing at me."

He let out a chuckle, walked over, and gripped my hips. "No, I wasn't. But if you want to believe it in that crazy little head of yours, go ahead. I have to go." His lips pressed against my forehead, and my brows furrowed.

"Why did you just do that?" I asked.

"I'm not sure." He smiled, grabbed his briefcase, and stepped into the elevator.

"Don't do it again!" I shouted.

"HE KISSED my forehead this morning before he left for work," I told Olivia as we walked down the street to the bookstore.

"Ah, that sexy McBillionaire. You loved it. Admit it." She shoulder-bumped me.

"I did not."

"You did, you liar."

"Okay, I did." We stepped into the bookstore and headed to the pregnancy section.

"I know the man likes you. What's not to like? You're beautiful, fun, smart, and pregnant with his babies. And we know you like him too. Perhaps you're falling in love with him." She pulled a book from the shelf.

"Stop your craziness. I am not falling in love with him. He's the father of my kids, and that's it."

"With whom you're regularly having sex with."

"So? We sleep in the same bed. Of course, things are going to happen. It's human nature. It means nothing."

"Whatever you say, my hormonal little minx."

I pulled a book from the shelf titled Holy Shit I'm Having Twins and thumbed through it.

"Here. This is for Daddy McBillionaire." Olivia handed me a book titled Dad's Guide to Having Twins.

"There is no way Charlie Stone will read this book. He doesn't even want his children."

"Just buy it. You never know. Maybe he'll surprise you," she said.

Grabbing a few more pregnancy books from the shelf, I took them up to the counter and checked out. The cashier smiled at me as she rang up each book.

"I can't believe fall is here already," Olivia said as we left the bookstore. "You're going to have to go shopping for clothes." A smirk crossed her lips. "No more baggy dresses for you. Leggings and oversized sweaters for the pregnant mama."

"Thanks for reminding me." I rolled my eyes.

When I arrived home, I took the books out of the bag. Setting my stack on my nightstand, I took the book for Charlie and put it on his. Wouldn't he be surprised when he got home?

I was a nervous wreck as I touched up my makeup and ran a brush through my hair. Telling my mother I was pregnant should have been exciting, but it wasn't. I was filled with nothing but dread.

"There you are," Charlie said. "Let me change my clothes really quick, and we'll go."

I followed him out of the bathroom and saw him walk over to his nightstand, pick up the book, and look at it.

"What's this?"

"I picked it up for you at the bookstore."

"I'm not reading this, Marley. There's no need."

"Whatever, Charlie. I don't really care. Olivia made me buy it." I walked out of the bedroom.

A few moments later, he emerged and asked if I was ready to go. We stepped into the elevator and headed to Long Island.

"What else did you do today besides going to the bookstore?" he asked.

"Why do you care?" I glanced at him.

"What's with the attitude, Marley?"

"I don't have an attitude, Charlie. You never ask about my day. And the one time you decide to, I don't feel like sharing."

"You're stressed about having to tell your mother about your pregnancy, aren't you?"

"I have a doctor's appointment tomorrow, and I'd like you to be there," I said, changing the subject.

"Why are you just telling me this now? I can't tomorrow."

"That's fine."

Mateo pulled up to my mother's house, and I sighed.

"Let's get this over with."

I opened the door and stepped inside. My mother walked into the foyer and stopped when she saw Charlie.

"Marley, it's good to see you." She hugged me. "Who's this?"

"Mom, Charlie. Charlie, Maddie, my mother."

"It's nice to meet you, Charlie." She extended her hand.

"The pleasure is all mine." A smile graced his face as he placed his hand in hers.

"You look like you've put on some weight since the last time I saw you," my mother said.

"Thanks, Mom. I appreciate it." I rolled my eyes and went into the kitchen.

"Hi, Marley." Peter walked over and hugged me.

"Hey, Peter. This is Charlie. Charlie, Peter."

They shook hands, and my mother announced dinner was ready. We gathered in the dining room and took our seats at the table.

"I made your favorites." She smiled.

"Thanks, Mom."

I picked up the bowl of grilled asparagus, set it down, and placed my hand over my mouth.

"Excuse me." I flew out of my seat and ran to the bathroom.

When I was finished, I sat back down, noting the look on my mother's face.

"Are you okay?" she asked.

"I'm pregnant, Mom." I yelled out to get it over with.

"Pregnant?" She cocked her head. "I didn't know you were dating anyone. Is Charlie the father?"

"Yes, he's the father. And that's not all. I'm having twins. Thank you very much for telling me that twins run in our family." I picked up a glass of water and took a sip.

"Twins?" Peter smiled. "That's wonderful. Congratulations to the both of you."

"Marley, I don't know what to say. Are the two of you planning on getting married?"

"Does it matter?" I furrowed my brows as Charlie sat there in awkward silence, eating his dinner.

"Well, no. Congratulations. I can't believe I'm going to be a grandmother. How long have the two of you been dating?"

"We're not dating. It happened one drunken night. I just thought you should meet him."

After we ate, Charlie went with Peter into the living room while I helped my mother clean up the kitchen.

"You know I'm here for you, Marley," my mother said.

"I know, Mom." I placed the plates in the dishwasher.

"It hurts me that we don't see each other very often. I hope that will change when the twins are born. Even after all these years, I know you're still angry with me. I'm not stupid."

"I never said you were, Mom."

"At some point, you have to forgive me. You act like you had such a terrible childhood."

"Seeing your mother in bed with someone other than your father is pretty traumatic. And then being told not to tell Dad was even worse." I looked over and saw Charlie standing there staring at me.

My mother turned her back and walked over to the sink. "I've apologized to you for that."

"Thanks for dinner, Mom. It was really good." I grabbed my purse. "Come on, Charlie."

"You never told me you found your mother in bed with Peter," he said as we climbed into the backseat of the car.

"I was supposed to go to Penelope's house after school, but her mom came down with the flu that day. So, I went home. When I walked into the house, I couldn't find my mom anywhere, which I thought was odd because her car was there. I heard noises coming from upstairs, so I quietly walked up and stood outside her bedroom door. When I opened it, I saw them in the middle of having sex. My mom's eyes widened when she saw me. I shut the door and ran to my room, crying and not being able to understand what was happening. My mom came in shortly after and told me that she made a mistake and that my dad could never find out. She told me that if I told him, it would destroy our family, and it would be all my fault."

"You told him, anyway, didn't you?" Charlie reached over and grabbed hold of my hand.

"Yeah. I did. But not until two months later. It ate away at me every day I kept her secret. To give your eleven-year-old daughter that kind of responsibility was wrong on so many levels. The last thing I wanted to do was hurt my dad, but he needed to know. So, one day, I asked him if he could take me to the park. I told him what I saw, and I'll never forget the look on his face. Tears fell from his eyes, and he hugged me tight, telling me it wasn't my fault and everything would be okay. When we got home, he told me to go up to my room. I acted like I would but sat on the top step as he confronted her. There was a lot of screaming and crying. My dad flew up the stairs, packed his suitcase, kissed me on the head, and left."

"I'm sorry, Marley."

"So now you know even more why I don't have a great relationship with my mother."

"It's totally understandable." His hand squeezed mine.

Chapter Twenty

CHARLIE

The following morning, I was in the shower when the door opened, and Marley stepped in.

"Sorry, but I need to take a quick shower. I have a lot of things to do today."

"You do know that you standing there naked is not going to get you out of this shower fast."

"I'm not in the mood, Charlie."

"You're not?" A smirk crossed my lips as my hands groped her breasts.

"No." She closed her eyes.

Wrapping one arm around her waist and holding her in my grip, I dipped a finger inside her.

"How about now?"

"Oh God," she moaned.

"And now?" My lips wrapped around her hardened peaks.

Her hand wrapped around my hard cock and stroked it up and down as the hot water beat down on us.

"I need to be inside you right now," I whispered as my tongue trailed across her neck.

"Then, by all means, enter."

With a growl, I turned her around, and she placed her hands firmly against the tiled wall. Taking my cock, I thrust inside her as moans escaped both of our lips. With a slight turn of her head, our lips met as I moved in and out of her with my arm securely holding her. Her orgasm gripped me, and I exploded. We stood there for a moment, breathless, as I strained, making sure every last drop I had was inside her. I loosened my grip, and my hand stopped on her belly. I felt the bump, and my hand froze.

"Are you okay?" she asked as I stood there, not moving.

"Yeah. I'm great." I kissed the side of her neck and pulled out of her.

I finished my shower first and climbed out. Wrapping a towel around my waist, I gripped the sink and stared at her as she washed her hair. Swallowing hard, I finished getting ready for work.

"What time is your doctor's appointment?" I asked.

"Two o'clock. Why?"

"I suppose I can meet you there."

"You don't have to, Charlie. I know you're busy. Don't worry about it." She walked past me.

"I said I'll meet you there," I spoke in a commanding tone.

"Okay. If you really want to. I'll text you the address."

"Okay." I grabbed my briefcase. I'll see you later."

I was sitting in my office when a call came through from Grant.

"Hey, Grant."

"Hey, Charlie. I found an apartment that I think you'll really like. Do you have time to see it today?"

"What time were you thinking?" I asked.

"Around three o'clock."

"I have an appointment at two o'clock, and I'm not sure how long it will take. How about I text you when I leave my appointment?"

"Sounds good. I'll talk to you later."

"Was that Grant's voice I heard?" Chase's brows furrowed when he walked into my office.

"Yeah."

"You planning on moving again?"

"No. I'm having him look for an apartment for Marley."

"Oh. Does she know?" He took a seat.

"No. Not yet."

"I thought things were going good between you two," he said.

"Things are okay."

"Then why are you kicking her out?"

I stared at him and didn't say a word.

"Enough of this crap, Charlie. I know exactly what's going on here."

"You don't know shit, Chase."

"Yeah. I do. You're falling in love with her, if you're not already, and freaking the fuck out."

"I am not in love with her."

"Yes, you are, my friend. Fuck. Just admit it. Stop trying to deny it. Loving someone is being human. You're human, Charlie. As I've said before, I know the reason you are the way you are. You don't think I know, but I do."

"And like I said. You don't know shit."

"Fuck, I do, man." He shook his head. "Do you remember back in college when you were fucking that chick named Grace, and she told you that she loved you, and you flipped out on her?"

"Barely. If I recall, I was a drunken mess that night."

"You were, and I picked your ass up off the steps of our dorm and took you back to our room. You told me that love will never be part of the deal for you in your lifetime because you're too scared of losing someone like you did with your parents. You said that the pain and suffering of losing someone you so deeply love isn't worth it and that you will never allow it to happen again because you can't control what happens in the outside world, but you can control your feelings and emotions."

I stared at him in shock because I had no idea I'd ever spoken those words to him.

"So when I tell you that I know why you're fighting your feelings about Marley and the twins, I know what the fuck I'm talking about."

I brought my hand up and ran it down my face.

"It's too much, Chase. Too fucking much. I'm not denying I have feelings for Marley because I do. But I can't be a father."

"But you can be. You're just too scared of what might happen. It's not because you had a bad father figure. From what you told me, your father was an amazing man, and the two of you were very close. He was your role model, Charlie. God, I can only imagine what he's thinking about you right now up in Heaven and hearing you say this shit. You told me he and your mother were always so proud of you and showed it. Do you think they'd be proud of you now?"

"Shut the fuck up."

"No, I won't. It's the goddamn truth, and you know it." He pointed at me.

"Why didn't you ever tell me what I said to you that night?" I asked.

"Because I knew you would never say that sober, and I didn't want to upset you. So, I kept it to myself until I knew when the time was right to use it. Now is that time."

"You're an asshole." I shook my head.

"I know." He grinned, standing up from his chair. "I'm your best friend, and I've stood by you all these years and watched you become a man who deserves so much more in life than just this company. I've never really said much to you about it, but now I am because the time has come, my friend, for you to step into reality and out of that place you've been hiding in since the death of your parents—the place of fear." He turned and walked out of my office.

Glancing at the time, I had to leave for Marley's doctor's appointment. Climbing into the back of the sedan, I gave Mateo the address.

When I opened the door to the practice, I saw Marley sitting in a chair. Walking over, I sat next to her and stared at all the pregnant women waiting. One man was sitting next to his wife, softly stroking her belly as she looked like she was about to give birth any day.

"If this is making you too nervous, you don't have to be here," Marley said.

"Nervous?" My brows furrowed. "No. I'm fine. You're the one who should be nervous."

"Why me?"

"Because you're pregnant with twins. I can only imagine how hard that will be delivering two babies." I smirked.

"No. No. No." She shook her head. "I'm having a C-section. There is no way these little ruga roos are coming out of my vagina."

"Marley?" The nurse called her name.

We stood up and followed her back to a room. After she took Marley's blood pressure, she told her the doctor would be in soon. I sat in the chair and stared at the pictures on the wall. I never thought I'd be sitting in an OB/GYN office with a woman in a million years. But here I was.

"How is Mama doing today?" The doctor smiled, walking into the room. "Oh, hello. Dr. Gregario." He extended his hand.

"Charlie." I lightly shook it.

"Father?"

"Yes."

"Very good." He smiled. "So, Marley. How are you feeling?"

"Still nauseous all day, not vomiting as much, but still tired."

"Well, that's to be expected. Lie down on the table and lift up your shirt," he said. "Ah, look at that. The baby bump has appeared."

"Isn't it kind of early?" Marley asked him.

"Not with twins. We're going to draw your blood and run some genetic tests to make sure there aren't any abnormalities."

"What do you mean?" I asked.

"We're testing for genetic disorders. It's just a precaution. We'll also be able to find out the twins' genders if you're interested. After you get your blood drawn, Marley, the nurse will take you down to the ultrasound room, and we'll see what your babies are up to." He smiled.

Chapter Twenty-One

CHARLIE

The door opened to the ultrasound room, and Dr. Gregario walked in.

"Okay, let's see how the babies are cooking in there." He grinned.

I furrowed my brows at Marley because I felt this guy was a little off. I stared at the monitor as the doctor moved the wand across Marley's belly. My heart started to race.

"Ah, look at those little beauties. Here's Baby A and Baby B. Do you want to know if they're identical or fraternal?" Dr. Gregario asked.

"Yes," Marley replied. "I need to know in advance if my stress levels are going to rise because I won't be able to tell my babies apart."

I swallowed hard as I reached over and took hold of her hand.

"Your stress levels are going to be just fine, Marley. Your babies are fraternal twins."

"Oh, thank God." She sighed in relief, and I gently squeezed her hand.

"The babies look great and are growing on schedule." Dr. Gregario grinned. "Keep up the good work, Marley. If you should experience any issues before your next appointment, be sure to call me. It's better to be safe than sorry. If you haven't already, I suggest you go and get some books on twin pregnancies. Knowledge is your superpower."

"Thanks, Dr. Gregario." Marley smiled.

He printed the ultrasound pictures and handed them to her.

"I'll see you next month." He walked out of the room.

"Are you heading home?" I asked her as we walked out of the building.

"I have a couple of errands to run."

"I have another appointment to get to. I'll have Mateo drive you, and I'll take a cab." I opened the door to the sedan. "Mateo, Marley has errands to run. Take her to wherever she needs to go."

"Will do, Charlie." Mateo smiled.

"I'll see you later," I told her as I shut the door.

Pulling my phone from my pocket, I texted Grant.

"I can meet now if you're available."

"Excellent. I'm actually over that way. I'll text you the address."

I hailed a cab and met Grant outside the apartment building. We took the elevator up to the sixteenth floor, opened the apartment door, and stepped inside.

"This one just went on the market this morning," Grant said.

Tucking my hands into my pants pockets, I looked around. "It's nice."

"It's a great neighborhood, has good schools, and great views. The owner's job transferred him to their Los Angeles office, so he had to move rather quickly. It is available for immediate move-in."

I walked around the space, checking out each bedroom

and bathroom. A nauseous feeling filled my stomach as I stared out the window overlooking the city.

"Are you okay, Charlie?" Grant asked.

"I don't know." I sighed. "I really don't." I turned and stared at him. "I'm sorry, my friend, for wasting your time. As nice as this apartment is, it's not right."

"You've changed your mind about buying an apartment?" A smirk crossed Grant's lips.

"Yeah. I have."

He walked over and placed his hand on my shoulder. "I'm happy you're not going through with it. Everything will be okay, Charlie."

"Thanks, Grant."

As I was walking down the hall, I stopped in Chase's office and shut the door.

"What's up?" He smiled.

"I went and saw that apartment." I sat on his couch.

He stood up from behind his desk, walked over, and sat next to me. "And?"

"Marley had an ultrasound today."

"Ah, so you saw your babies?"

"Yeah, and I heard their heartbeats. Everything suddenly became real."

"What about the apartment?" he asked.

"I told Grant I'm not going through with it."

"Thank God." Chase sighed, placing his hand on my shoulder. "You're overthinking this whole situation, Charlie. Just feel your feelings. Don't fight them anymore."

I inhaled a sharp breath as I stood up. "I'll talk to you later."

~

MARLEY

I finished my errands and had Mateo drop me off at Love At First Sip. Walking through the door, Olivia and Penelope looked up and ran over to me.

"How did your appointment go?" Penelope asked, grabbing my hand and leading me to a table.

I reached into my purse and pulled out the ultrasound pictures.

"Baby A and Baby B."

"Damn, look at those little future troublemakers." Olivia grinned.

"They already look beautiful." Penelope smiled.

"So, how did Daddy McBillionaire react," Olivia said.

"He didn't say much, but I didn't expect him to. He's really good at hiding his emotions."

"Sounds like someone else I know." Olivia cocked her head.

I rolled my eyes. "I'm starving. Can you two escape here so we can go get some dinner?"

"You bet." Penelope smiled. "Just give us a few minutes."

My heart started racing as I stared at the sonogram pictures. The babies had grown since my last ultrasound and were beginning to look like real little humans. I started to question everything in my head. How was I going to take care of both of them at once? Would I be a good Mom? Would I fail them somehow? Would I know what to do if they got sick?

The girls and I went to dinner and walked around the city until it started pouring. We shared a cab, and the driver dropped me off first. When I stepped off the elevator, it was nine o'clock.

"Where the fuck were you?" Charlie shouted.

"I was at dinner with Penelope and Olivia." My brows furrowed as I set my purse down.

"I tried calling you a million times, and it kept going straight to voicemail!"

"My phone died earlier. What is going on here? Who do you think you are speaking to me that way?" I stormed into the bathroom and started the bath water.

"I was worried something happened to you!" he shouted. "I couldn't reach you, so I called Mateo, and he said he dropped you off at Love At First Sip hours ago."

"Okay, then you knew I was with Olivia and Penelope," I said.

"No, I didn't know that, Marley!"

I'd never seen him as angry as he was. "You need to chill, Charlie." I plugged my phone into the charger and set it on the nightstand.

"Don't you dare tell me to chill. I was worried."

I turned and stared into his angry eyes.

"Worried about what?"

"That something happened to you. I want you to share your location with me so I know where you're at, at all times."

"Ha, you're crazy."

"Do you think I'm joking?"

"I'm not discussing this now. I'm tired, and I want to take a bath." I went into the bathroom and twisted up my hair.

"How could you be so irresponsible and let your phone die?" he asked.

"It happens."

He walked over and gripped my arms. "You just don't get it," he spoke through gritted teeth as his eyes stared into mine.

At that moment, I saw something unexplainable in him. He let go of my arms and embraced me tightly. Bringing my hands up to his back, I softly stroked it, unsure of what was going on. I glanced over at the tub and noticed the water was at the edge.

"Um, Charlie? The tub is going to overflow any second."

"Shit." He ran over, turned the water off, pulled the drain, and walked out of the bathroom.

"What is going on here?" I walked into the bedroom and threw my hands up in the air.

"Just go take your bath." He sat on the edge of the bed with his head lowered.

"Can't now that you let the water go down the drain."

"I'll go refill it." He stood up, and I grabbed his arm as he began walking away.

"Forget the bath. It's obvious you're having a meltdown of some sort, and I want to know what your problem is."

"You really want to know what my problem is, Marley? I care. Okay? There, I said it."

"Care about?" I cocked my head.

He inhaled a sharp breath as his eyes stared into mine.

"I care about you and those children you're carrying."

"You mean *your* children." I arched my brow.

"Yeah, my children." He sighed, running his hand through his hair.

Chapter Twenty-Two

CHARLIE

My heart was pounding out of my chest. I wasn't any good at talking about my feelings since my parents died, and I didn't know how to.

"What do you mean you 'care?'" she asked.

"I'm not any good at this, Marley." I paced around the bedroom. "I spent so many years on auto-pilot living my life. This wasn't supposed to happen—not to me. I had it all figured out."

"Had what figured out, Charlie?"

"How to walk away and not get involved. How to not feel anything. But then you had to sit down next to me at that airport in Chicago and ramble on and on about your upgrade to first class. Then your seat just so happened to be next to mine. Then we make it back to New York, and I run into you at the coffee shop. And the fucking icing on the cake was that your friend just so happened to be the cousin of one of my employees, and you show up at my housewarming party. Then we slept together, and you got pregnant."

"Don't forget the Lake's party, and you took me to dinner, and we slept together again."

"Trust me. I haven't forgotten. I haven't forgotten one single moment we spent together."

"But then you were a douchebag and didn't call me for a month."

"Because I knew!"

"Knew what?"

"Knew there was something about you that I couldn't control!" I shouted.

"You were trying to control me?" Her brows furrowed.

"No, Marley. Not you. The feelings that I felt for you. I wanted to distance myself because it was happening. That's why I didn't call you. I couldn't let it happen."

"Charlie." She walked over and placed her hand on my back.

"I was scared enough, and then you burst in here and tell me you're pregnant and that I'm the father. After your doctor's appointment today, I met with my realtor, Grant, and looked at an apartment that I was going to buy for you and the twins. But I couldn't do it as I stood inside that apartment."

"First of all, I can't believe you did that, and second, why?"

"Because you belong here with me. You and our children belong here with me, in this penthouse."

"And if I don't want to stay here?"

"You don't have a choice. You're not going anywhere. Listen, Marley." I held her hand and led her to the bed, where we sat down. "I'm going to ask you something and need an honest answer."

"Okay."

"Do you have feelings for me?"

She stared into my eyes, and I could see the tears fill inside hers. "I'm not good at this kind of stuff, Charlie."

"Neither am I. Answer my question."

"Ye—Ye—" Her bottom lip trembled. "Yes."

I inhaled a sharp breath, wrapped my arms around her, and pulled her into me.

"How could you do this to me?" she asked.

"Do what to you?" I softly stroked the back of her head.

"Make me admit it out loud?"

I let out a light chuckle. "If I had to, then so did you."

She broke our embrace. "I don't understand why you're so angry that you couldn't get a hold of me."

"It all stems from my parent's death. I can't control what happens out there in the world, and I hate it. I was worried something bad happened to you and the twins. Call me overprotective. I don't care. It's something I need to work on."

"I can maybe help you with that." She smiled, bringing her hand to my cheek. "So now what?"

"I think we're on the same page as far as feelings go for each other, and we should take it slow and one day at a time," I said, softly stroking her hair. "I know you don't believe in love after your parents, but we're our own people, Marley. You need to get over it, as do I. Maybe we can help each other see the brighter side."

"You think?" she asked.

"Yeah. I do." I smiled as my lips brushed against hers. "Are you going to share your location with me?"

"Are you?" Her brow arched.

"You bet." A grin crossed my lips. "I have nothing to hide."

"And neither do I. So, are we just going to sit here all

night, or are you going to fuck me senseless after we just poured our feelings out to each other?"

"I love it when you talk dirty." I pushed her down on the bed and kissed her passionately.

MARLEY

I woke up in his arms, our bodies tangled with each other's as his alarm went off. Rolling over, he shut it down and wrapped his arms around me again, kissing my head.

"I have to get up and get ready for work."

"I know." I quickly sat up, placed my hand over my mouth for a moment, and then pulled it away. "False alarm."

His lips formed a smile as he kissed me and climbed out of bed. While he was in the shower, I went into the kitchen and made him a cup of coffee and me a decaf. Glancing at the island, I saw an invitation sitting there, so I picked it up.

"You're invited to Miles Bradshaw's surprise party?" I asked when he walked into the kitchen.

"Yeah. It just came yesterday. You're going with me."

"I hate to burst your little control bubble, but I'll already be there."

"What are you talking about?" He picked up his coffee cup and brought it to his lips.

"I'm the one who planned this little party with Stella."

"Seriously?" His brows furrowed. "You didn't tell me that."

"I guess it never came up. You were doing your thing, and I was doing mine."

He walked over and gripped my hips. "I think we need to communicate more." He kissed my forehead. "I'll see you later." He walked toward the elevator and stopped. "How about we go out tonight? Anywhere you want to go and want to do."

"Really?" I smiled.

"Yeah, really." He winked.

After showering and getting dressed, I headed to Love At First Sip.

"Hey, Mama." Olivia smiled.

"Hey, you. Where's Penelope?"

"Dentist appointment." Her eyes narrowed at me. "What's going on with you?"

"What do you mean?" I cocked my head.

"Something is different. You're a mix of happy yet nervous. I'm going to make you a raspberry lemonade surprise, and we're going to have a little chat."

"Could we go to that ice cream place down the street instead? I'm craving ice cream really bad right now."

"You got it." Olivia grinned. "You two keep an eye on the shop. I'll be back," Olivia said to her two employees, hooked her arm around me, and we walked out of the shop.

After getting our ice cream, we sat down at a table. Pushing my spoon into my triple chocolate sundae, I closed my eyes as I shoved it in my mouth, and the delicacy of chocolate soothed me. Olivia's brow furrowed as she watched me.

"You're freaking me out. What happened?"

"When I got home last night, Charlie screamed at me. He wanted to know where I was because he'd been trying to call me."

"Did you tell him your phone died?"

"Yeah, and it just escalated from there." I took another bite of my sundae. "He told me he wanted me to share my location with him."

"Oh, hell no," Olivia said. "He doesn't get that right."

"Wait." I held up my finger. "Once he calmed down, we had a long talk. He told me he had feelings for me and wanted to know if I did for him."

"Wow. What did you tell him?"

"I finally said yes once the word could finally come out." I sighed. "I think we may be a couple now."

"You think?" Her brows furrowed. "What do you mean you think?"

I told her everything he said to me about his feelings and the death of his parents. I also told her about the apartment he looked at and then changed his mind about.

"Why are we getting ice cream so early in the day?" Penelope asked, walking over to our table. "I couldn't believe when I checked your location, you two were here."

"Preggo over here needed it. Sit down. McBillionaire confessed his feelings to our girl last night, and she's freaking out," Olivia said.

"What? Oh, my God!" Penelope pulled up a chair and placed her hand on mine. "That's wonderful, Mar. Why are you freaking out?"

"I'm not freaking out. It's just—"

"Your parents caused a traumatic event in your life, and you think everyone is like that." Olivia pursed her lips and cocked her head.

"I can't help it."

"Are you in love with him?" Penelope asked.

"Yeah, and I'm terrified of it. My life has changed so quickly. I went from being this single woman who didn't have a care in the world about guys to getting pregnant with twins and falling in love with a broken man."

"A broken billionaire." Olivia pointed at me. "Who cares if he's broken? He's rich and sexy. Besides, you're broken, too. You're two broken people who fell in love, trying to navigate pending parenthood and life. The two of you couldn't be more suited for each other."

"He's taking me out tonight." I smiled.

"Where are you two going?"

"I don't know. He said it's up to me, anything I want to do."

"He's dreamy." Penelope smiled. "I want a McBillion-aire." A pout formed on her lips.

"He is, isn't he?" I smiled as I finished my sundae.

Chapter Twenty-Three

CHARLIE

I was looking over the coding for a new game in development when Chase walked into my office.

"Here are the reports for the last quarter." He grinned. "I think you're going to like what you see."

I took the report from his hand and reviewed it.

"Damn. We beat out the last quarter." I smiled.

"We sure did. So, what time did Marley get home last night?"

"Around nine o'clock."

"I hope you weren't too hard on her."

"I was at first. We talked, and I told her how I felt. I told her everything, Chase."

"And how did it feel?"

"It felt good. We're taking it slow and one day at a time."

"You have no idea how proud I am of you." A smile crossed his lips. "Doesn't it feel good?"

I chuckled. "Yeah. It does." I picked up my phone and furrowed my brows when I checked Marley's location.

"What's wrong?"

"Marley is at an ice cream shop."

"And? She's pregnant."

"Isn't it kind of early for ice cream?" I looked at him.

"Isn't it kind of weird you're being a damn stalker?"

"You're right." I sighed, setting my phone down.

After I left the office, I headed straight home. When I stepped off the elevator, I set my briefcase down and walked into the kitchen, where I saw some shopping bags sitting on the island.

"What's all this?" I asked, gripping her hips and kissing her lips.

"The last things I needed for the Bradshaw birthday bash." A beautiful smile crossed her face.

I stared into her eyes and pushed a strand of her hair behind her ear.

"What?" she asked.

"I kind of missed you today."

"I kind of missed you too." She grinned.

"Did you decide what you wanted to do tonight?"

"I have." She wrapped her arms around my neck. "I want to get hot dogs from a hot dog stand on the street and eat them while we ride through Central Park on a horse and carriage."

"That sounds like a good plan." I kissed her forehead. "I'll reserve a horse and carriage for us online."

"I already did, Charlie."

"You did?"

"Yeah. I couldn't risk them selling out."

"Then you should have told me earlier, and I would have done it. How much was it?" I pulled my wallet from my suit coat.

"I'm not telling you, and you're not paying. I am. It's my treat tonight. You can pay for the hot dogs."

"We'll discuss it later. Let me change out of this suit, and we'll head out."

"I'm going to change too. It's kind of chilly out."

As I removed my suit, I watched her put on a pair of black leggings and an oversized NYU sweatshirt. I smiled, and she caught me.

"What?" A grin crossed her lips.

"You look adorable in that outfit."

"You're sweet. You don't think I'm way underdressed, right?"

"Not at all. In fact, I think I might wear a pair of sweatpants and a sweatshirt, too."

"Seriously? You, Charlie Stone, would go out around the city in a pair of sweatpants and a sweatshirt?"

"Yeah. Why not?" I winked.

We headed down to the lobby, where Mateo was waiting for us. When we stepped out the door, he smiled.

"Love the casual look, Charlie. I'm not sure I've ever seen you leave the penthouse in clothes like those."

"Thank you, Mateo. Marley and I are having a very casual night."

"Excellent. Where to?" he asked, climbing into the car.

"Billy's Hot Dog Cart and then to the horse and carriages at Central Park." Marley grinned.

"You heard the beautiful woman, Mateo." I smirked, grabbing Marley's hand.

We stood in line at the hot dog cart, and I asked her what she wanted.

"Two hot dogs with relish and a pretzel. Oh, and a bottle of water."

"Two hot dogs and a pretzel?" My brow arched.

"Hello, I'm eating for three."

I chuckled as I kissed the side of her head. After

receiving our order, we walked over to where the horses and carriages were.

"Good evening. How are you lovely folks tonight?"

"We're great." Marley smiled, pulling out her phone. "We have reservations."

"Excellent. Climb aboard."

I held all the hot dogs, pretzels, and bottled water while Marley climbed into the carriage. Sitting next to her, I handed her two hot dogs with relish and her pretzel.

"This might be kind of messy," I said.

"It's okay. Whatever we get on our clothes will come off in the wash." She smiled.

The horse and carriage ride started. It was a chilly night but calm and peaceful. There was no place else I'd rather be.

"I've been to this park a thousand times, and tonight, it feels like I'm seeing it for the first time," Marley said.

"That's because you're with me." I winked.

"True." She leaned in and kissed my cheek.

Two Weeks Later

MARLEY

I stared at him as he peacefully slept, watching the subtle rise and fall of his chest with each breath. There was no doubt that I was in love with him. For the first time in my life, I let my emotions and feelings escape the grip I'd held them in all these years. I wasn't looking for anyone or anything, but here I was, in love with this man and having his babies.

I sat up in bed, hoping the horrific heartburn I'd felt would diminish. Placing my hand on my belly, the babies grew overnight. The alarm went off. Charlie rolled over and shut it down, then rolled back and smiled at me.

"What are you doing?"

"Heartburn. Bad heartburn."

"I'm sure those large chili cheese fries you ate before bed last night didn't help." A smirk crossed his lips.

"Why did you let me eat them?" I asked, cocking my head.

"Like I could stop you." He sat up, kissed my lips, and climbed out of bed.

"All you had to do was take them away from me!" I shouted as he went into the bathroom.

"And risk getting kicked in the balls? I don't think so."

Climbing out of bed, I went to the kitchen and pulled the antacids out of the cabinet, praying they would work fast.

"Wow," Charlie said, walking into the kitchen. "Your belly expanded overnight."

"It's from the chili cheese fries." I smirked.

"Ah, okay. If you say so." He picked up the cup of coffee I'd made him from the island.

"So, before you leave for work, let's talk about your sperm."

"What about them?" His brow arched.

"You know your sperm determines the sex of our children, right?"

"Yes. I'm aware." He tipped the cup to his lips, leaning against the island, staring at me.

"So, what gender do you think our babies are?"

"Honestly, I haven't given it any thought. But we will find out tonight at the gender reveal party."

"What do you want?" I asked out of curiosity.

"It doesn't matter. As long as they're healthy."

"Good answer. Me too. But, wouldn't one of each be nice?"

"Yes, one of each would be nice. Or two boys or two girls. It really doesn't matter to me." He set his cup down and kissed my lips. "I have to go. I'll see you later." His lips tenderly brushed mine.

"Have a good day." I smiled.

As he headed toward the elevator, he stopped and turned to me. "If one of the babies happens to be a girl, no boys will be coming around until she's at least twenty-one."

"You think so?" I arched my brow.

"I know so." He winked.

When I had my last doctor's appointment to go over the genetic test results, Dr. Gregario handed us a sealed envelope with the genders of our twins. I handed it over to Olivia since she and Penelope wanted to do a gender reveal for us. The party would be at Chase and Lila's penthouse, and the three of them had been in cahoots planning it. Even though event planning was my thing, they wouldn't allow me to do anything. It was going to be the six of us. Penelope thought we should have invited my mom and dad. I shot that down immediately. Having the two of them in the same room with each other's exes was stressful, and I didn't need that.

As I was running some errands, my phone pinged with a text from Olivia.

"Six o'clock, sharp. DO NOT BE LATE!"

"You don't need to tell me. You need to tell Charlie that."

"I already did. He said not to worry."

"Then we'll be there at six sharp. Maybe we'll even be there five minutes early."

Just as I put my phone in my purse, it rang. Pulling it back out, I saw a number that was unfamiliar.

"Hello."

"Hi, is this Marley Monroe?"

"Yes. This is she."

"Hi, Marley. My name is Allison, and I got your number from a friend of mine. I just recently got engaged and would love to talk to you about planning our wedding."

"Congratulations, Allison. I'd love to talk to you. What day and time were you thinking?"

"Is tomorrow at noon okay? I'd love to meet at my home, but we're doing some renovations, and it's a mess.

"Tomorrow at noon is perfect. We can meet at my house. I'll text you the address."

"Sounds good. Thank you, Marley. I'll see you tomorrow."

I ended the call with a smile. "Yay, me! A wedding."

Chapter Twenty-Four

MARLEY

When I arrived home, I saw Charlie's briefcase in the foyer. Glancing at my watch, it was only four o'clock.

"Charlie?" I shouted.

"In my office."

I set my bags on the island and went into his office, where he sat on the couch, playing a video game.

"You're home way early." I smiled, wrapping my arms around his neck from behind and kissing his cheek.

"I was at a meeting not too far from here, and I figured I could do the rest of my work from home since Olivia threatened me about being late for the party. I didn't want to take any chances."

"I'm surprised you didn't text me and ask where I was."

"I knew where you were. Did you have fun at Target?"

"Stalker." I walked around and sat beside him.

"If you were stalking me, you would have known I was home." A smirk crossed his lips.

"True. I guess it slipped my mind. See, I would only

stalk you if you were supposed to be home at a certain time and you weren't." I ran my fingers across the back of his head.

"Fuck! This isn't right." He scowled, pulling out his phone.

"New game?"

"Yeah. I swear I'm firing Lenny." He sighed.

"Don't be a meanie." I kissed his cheek. "I'm going to change for the party." I stood up from the couch. "Oh, guess what?"

"What?" His eyes diverted up to me.

"I got a phone call today from a woman named Allison. She's coming by the penthouse tomorrow at noon to discuss my planning her upcoming nuptials." I grinned.

"That's great news. Congratulations, babe."

"Thank you."

"Um, one thing," he said.

"Yes?"

"Why does she have to come here?"

"I don't know." I shrugged. "It's quiet, and I don't have to carry my portfolio and books with my prices."

"Where did you meet clients before you moved in here?"

"Why are you asking these questions?" My brows furrowed. "Do you have a problem with one of my clients coming here?"

"Yeah, a little bit. I don't want strangers in my home. You really should have asked me first."

"Right," I spoke with irritation. "I apologize, Mr. Stone. It won't happen again." I walked out of his office angry.

Grabbing my phone from my purse, I went into the bedroom and sent Allison a text.

"Hi, Allison. Change of location for our meeting tomorrow. I

forgot our cleaners will be here. I hope this location is okay with you. "
I sent her the address to Love At First Sip.

"Oh, I love that coffee shop! I'll see you tomorrow, Marley. "

In his home? HIS home. I thought it was our home, but I was mistaken. He walked into the bedroom as I was changing.

"I didn't like the way you left my office," he said. "You're pissed off at me. I can tell."

I turned and smiled at him. "I'm not mad at you, darling. It was wrong of me to invite a stranger into YOUR," I emphasized the word "home. It won't happen again. But to say I'm MAD IS AN UNDERSTATE-MENT!" I shouted as I walked past him.

He reached out, grabbed my arm, and pulled me into him.

"Are you finished?" He held my head against his chest.

"Maybe."

"I'm sorry, Marley. I really need you to understand that I don't want strangers coming in and out of the penthouse —our penthouse."

"Fine, Charley. I get it." I broke our embrace and placed my hands on the sides of his face. "I'm sorry I went psycho. It's hormones." I kissed his lips. "Normally, I meet my clients at their home, but Allison said their house is being renovated, and it's a mess, so my first thought was here."

"It's fine. She can come here tomorrow, but nobody else after her," he said.

"I already texted her and told her to meet me at Love At First Sip."

"Okay." He kissed my forehead. "Mateo will drive you and help you with your things. Let's get ready for the party, or Olivia will have both of our heads." He smirked.

I was in awe of the decorations when we stepped into

Chase and Lila's penthouse. Beautiful, tall floral arrangements made up of pink and baby blue carnations greeted us.

"Oh, my gosh." I smiled when we stepped into the living room and saw the rest of the decorations. "You three did this?"

"We learned from the best." Penelope grinned, hooking her arm around me.

"God knows I've been to enough of your events. I know what I'm doing." Olivia smiled.

"Whoa, Marley." Chase smiled. "I know I haven't seen you in a couple of weeks, but good lord." He pointed to my belly.

"They're growing fast." I smiled.

Lila asked everyone to take their seats for dinner. As soon as we finished the elegant meal the chef they brought in cooked for us, it was time to find out the gender of our babies.

"Come with me," Lila smiled, grabbing Charlie's and my hands. She led us over to the large archway decorated with pink and blue balloons. In front of the arch sat two oversized white boxes labeled Baby A and Baby B. "Marley, you stand behind box A, and Charlie, you stand behind box B. You will do this one at a time. No cheating and opening them together. Got it!" Lila pointed at us.

"Got it." I smiled.

"Let's find out what these McBillionaire babies are!" Olivia shouted.

"On the count of three, Marley, slowly lift the lid to your box," Penelope said.

"One, two, three!" They all shouted.

I glanced at Charlie and slowly lifted the lid, and several pink balloons rose up.

"It's a girl!" I placed my hands over my mouth as I stared at Charlie.

He wrapped his arms around me and held me tight. "Remember, no boys allowed until she's twenty-one," he whispered in my ear and then kissed my lips.

"Okay, Charlie. Your turn." Lila said.

"Boy! Boy! Boy!" Chase chanted.

"Shut up." Lila playfully smacked him.

I stood next to Charlie and took in a deep breath. He slowly lifted the lid, and several blue balloons rose up.

"YES!" Chase shouted.

"One of each, babe." Charlie grinned as he grabbed me and held me tight.

We continued our celebration with an exquisite cake. After talking for a while, it was time to head home. When we stepped inside our penthouse, I entered the living room and suddenly froze. My heart started rapidly beating, and I began hyperventilating.

"Marley!" Charlie ran over and gripped me. "What's wrong."

I stared at him with widened eyes as I couldn't breathe.

"Relax, babe. Breathe with me. You can do it. It's okay."

The sound of his voice calmed and soothed me. My heart started to slow, and my breathing returned to normal. He led me to the couch and gripped my hand.

"What happened?" he asked with worry.

"Oh, I get like that sometimes."

"You were having a panic attack. Why?"

"Because it just hit me that this," I placed my hand on my belly, "is real now."

"What are you talking about? It's been real since the day you found out you were pregnant," he said.

"But now we know the genders, Charlie. These little

148

humans inside me have been gender assigned: a girl and a boy. That makes them more real, and I'm scared." Tears began to fill my eyes.

He wrapped his arms around me and pulled me into him. "I understand how you feel. I'm scared, too. I don't know how to be a father."

"And I don't know how to be a mother. I mean, look at my role model. At least yours were perfect and in love. You have one up on me."

He chuckled, breaking our embrace. "You are going to be a great mom. And you know what?"

"What?"

"We'll figure it out together." He wiped the tear that fell down my cheek. "I don't think any first-time parents know what they're doing. We'll blend right in." He smiled.

"Thank you."

"For what?" His finger softly stroked my cheek.

"For calming me down and making me feel better."

"Well, my job as our children's father is to take excellent care of their mother." His lips tenderly met mine.

I WALKED into Love At First Sip, and Olivia pointed to a table in the corner, where a young woman with long blonde hair sat.

"Allison?"

"Marley?" She smiled. "It's so nice to meet you." She stood up, and we hugged.

I showed her my portfolio, and we went over pricing. She hired me on the spot and wanted to get started right away.

"We already booked the church and the place for the reception."

I wrote down her wedding date, the church's name, and the Waldorf Astoria. Since the wedding was going to take place in three months, we needed to get moving on the details and order the invitations.

"If you don't mind me asking. Why are you getting married so quickly?" I asked.

"My fiancé said he didn't want to wait to get married. In fact, he suggested we go to the court and do it, but I've always dreamed of a big wedding, and my parents would be so angry if we did that. They're very wealthy and have many social statuses and friends."

"And what does your fiancé do?"

"He's a financial advisor at Chase Morgan."

"Nice. I can meet with you and your fiancé tomorrow if you want to look at invitations," I said. "We really need to pick one out and get them ordered."

"My fiancé is out of town on a business trip for the next two weeks. My mom and I can meet with you."

"Sure, okay."

"We can meet at my mother's house tomorrow around eleven o'clock. Will that work?"

"Eleven is fine."

"Great. I'll see you then, Marley."

Chapter Twenty-Five

CHARLIE

I opened my eyes before the alarm went off and stared at Marley as she slept on her back, her belly sticking up under the sheets. I was in love with her but had yet to tell her. She blew into my life without warning. One minute, she was sitting next to me on a plane back to New York, and the next, she was standing in my living room telling me she was pregnant.

She told me her panic attack a couple of weeks ago was because after we found out the gender of the twins, it made them more real. Perhaps that's how I felt. If I said those three words, it would make us real. Shit. The more I thought about it, the more I felt like an asshole. I loved this woman who disrupted my perfect bachelor's life.

Reaching over, I placed my hand on her belly. Her eyes opened, and she stared into mine.

"What are you doing?" A soft smile crossed her lips.

"You grew overnight again." I smirked.

"It's a nightly thing now," she yawned.

The alarm went off. Reaching over, I shut it down and held my arm out.

"I need some cuddling before I get up and ready for work." I smiled.

She snuggled against me, laying her head on my chest. I thought about how much my parents would have loved her.

"I love you, Marley."

She lifted her head and stared at me.

"Really?"

"Yes, really." My brows furrowed. "I'm pretty sure you know I love you."

"Well, I wasn't sure because you never said it."

"I know, and for that, I'm sorry. It's just—"

"It would make all of this more real?" A smirk crossed her lips.

"That, and I know how you feel about love. I didn't want to scare you off. I'm not scaring you off, am I? Because, just for the record, it's too late."

"No. I love you too, Charlie. I've never felt this way about anyone before. You blew into my life, got me drunk, impregnated me with two children at the same time, and here we are."

"I didn't get you drunk. You did that all on your own." I tapped the end of her nose. "And as for me blowing into your life, I think you're confused. You blew into my life by sitting down next to me in the airport. You could have sat elsewhere but chose the seat next to me."

"I'm happy I did because you had me at first glance." She wrinkled her nose.

"I'm happy you did too." I brought my hand to her face and softly stroked her cheek. "I'm so in love with you."

"I'm so in love with you too." She leaned in and kissed my lips.

Later that evening, Marley and I went to dinner at Eleven Madison Park. As we ate, Marley reached across the table and touched my arm.

"Look who's sitting in that booth," she said.

I glanced over and noticed it was the man she'd had a one-night stand with in Chicago. He sat beside a woman with his arm around her, stealing small kisses.

"That must be his girlfriend," Marley said. "Cheating bastard."

"It's none of our business, babe. Finish your dinner."

"It is my business when he straight up lied to me, Charlie."

"That's in the past. Let it stay there."

"It's just I hate people who cheat."

"Really? Because just the other night, you cheated while playing one of my games. You looked up the cheat code." My brow arched.

"You know what I mean, mister."

I chuckled. "I know. Be a good girl, mind your business, finish your dinner, and then I'll take you for ice cream."

"Really?" Her face lit up.

"Of course. I know how you get if you don't get your nightly dose of ice cream."

"I'm not that bad."

"I beg to differ." I smirked.

MARLEY

I was running late to the bakery, where I was meeting Allison for some cake testing. When I stepped inside, I froze when the man she was with turned around. His eyes widened as he looked at my expanding belly.

"Marley, look who's here." Allison beamed with excitement. "This is my fiancé, Troy. Troy, I'd like you to meet the woman who is helping plan our wedding. This is Marley."

"It's nice to meet you." He nervously extended his hand.

"You too." My eyes narrowed as I placed my hand in his. "Allison told me you were on a business trip the past couple of weeks. When did you get back?"

"Uh, a couple of nights ago."

Allison's phone rang. "Oh, excuse me. I have to take this call. It's important." She smiled, stepping out of the bakery.

"You cheating, little bastard," I spoke through gritted teeth. "I saw you last night at Eleven Madison Park playing kissy face with some woman who isn't your fiancée!"

"I can't believe Allison hired you. She never told me your name. All she kept saying was, 'Our event planner.' What's going on here?" He pointed to my belly.

I could see the fear in his eyes, and I couldn't resist.

"I was going to call you, but I didn't know your last name or how to get in touch."

"Excuse me?" He spoke through gritted teeth. "Are you saying—"

"There's a ninety percent chance that the babies are yours."

"Babies?"

"Twins." I smiled.

"That's impossible. I used a condom!"

"Perhaps it broke. I wasn't on birth control."

"You're a liar."

"No. You're the liar!" I jammed my finger into his chest. "Why are you marrying Allison if you can't keep your dick in your pants?"

"It's complicated." He sighed.

Allison walked back into the bakery, and Troy and I immediately composed ourselves and smiled.

"What are you two talking about?" Allison grinned.

"I was just asking Marley how far along she was. Did you know she's having twins, babe?"

"Yeah. She told me. I can't wait until we have kids." A bright smile crossed her lips.

I wanted to throw up. Allison was perhaps the nicest girl I'd ever met, and she didn't deserve a scumbag like Troy. After doing some cake testing, the cheater and Allison picked what they wanted.

"Thanks, Marley. I'll talk to you later." Allison smiled.

"I'll meet you in the car, babe. I want to grab a few pastries for the office," Troy said. As soon as she walked out, he turned to me. "If you think for one second that I'm going to be a father to those kids, you're sadly mistaken. There is no way they're mine."

"Well, I did find out I was pregnant shortly after Chicago, and I didn't sleep with anyone else, so—"

"Stop it!" He pointed at me. "You are not going to fucking ruin my life."

I was laughing hysterically on the inside, watching this man squirm.

"Stay out of my life, Marley." He turned to the door.

"Now that I know who and where you are, I'll need some of your DNA."

"Excuse me?" He turned to me.

"To prove that you're the twin's father." I smiled. "How are you going to explain to your beautiful fiancée that you're a cheating bastard? You have no business marrying that sweet girl. She doesn't deserve someone like you or have done what you're doing to her."

He shook his head, opened the door, and left the bakery. With a smile, I approached the counter and purchased some pastries to take to Charlie's office. When I arrived, he stood from his desk and embraced me.

"What are you doing here?" he asked.

"I bring pastries." I held up the white box.

"Ah, thank you." His lips met mine.

"You are never going to believe what happened," I said.

"What happened?" He removed an apple turnover from the box.

"I met Allison's fiancé."

"Oh yeah? Is he a nice guy?"

"He's Troy!"

He stopped chewing and stared at me. "As in Chicago one-night stand Troy? The guy we saw last night with that woman?"

"Yep." I popped my lips.

"Shit. What an asshole." He leaned against his desk. "What did he say when he saw you?"

"He was shocked. But even more shocked when he saw this." I placed my hand on my belly and twisted my face.

Charlie cocked his head. "Marley, what did you do?"

"It was too good of an opportunity to pass up, Charlie," I whined.

"Marley, what did you do?"

"I may have led him to believe the twins are his."

"WHAT?" he shouted.

"Calm down. I couldn't help it. You should have seen him. He was nervous and all squirmy. It's what he gets for lying to me to get me to sleep with his dumb, non-single ass."

"You can't fuck with people's lives like that. Wait a second. You didn't realize who he was when Allison gave you his name for the wedding invitations?"

"No. I didn't put two and two together. I didn't know

his last name, and hundreds of men could be named Troy in this city."

He ran his hand down his face and sighed.

"Don't be mad. Allison is the sweetest girl I've ever met, and she doesn't deserve this. He will cheat on her for the rest of his life. You saw how he was with the woman who was not his fiancée in the restaurant. I asked him why he's even marrying Allison, and you know what he said?"

"What?"

"He said it's complicated."

"Then he must be marrying her for some other reason," Charlie said.

"Can you find out?" I ran my finger down his chest. "Maybe hire a private investigator to do some digging."

"Are you serious?"

"Yes." I pouted.

"I may know someone who can find something out."

"This is why I love you so much." I grinned, kissing his lips.

Chapter Twenty-Six

CHARLIE

"Morgan." I smiled when she stepped into my office. Getting up from my desk, I walked over and hugged her. "It's great to see you. I was shocked when I heard you moved back to New York."

"Charlie Stone. It's great to see you too. It's been a while.

"Yeah, it has. Things didn't work out in Seattle?"

"No. It was too rainy there for me. Besides, I met a guy, and let's say he wasn't who I thought he was."

"I'm sorry. Have a seat, please. Can I get you some coffee?"

"I'm good. Thanks. So, to what do I owe the pleasure?"

"I need a favor."

"Okay. What is it?"

"I need someone checked out."

A smile crossed her lips. "Charlie Stone wants me to spy on someone for him?"

"It's for my girlfriend."

I told Morgan the story about how Marley and I met and about Troy.

"I want to meet her. She sounds like my kind of girl." She grinned.

"Perhaps we can have dinner together." I smiled.

"I'd love that. Write down the name of this Troy guy, and I'll dig up everything I can on him."

"Thanks, Morgan. I really appreciate this."

"Anything for you, my friend."

"By the way," I said as she walked to the door. "I don't want to know how you find out the information you're going to find." I smirked.

"No worries. You know I keep my secrets." She winked.

Later that evening, as the elevator approached the penthouse, I heard music blaring. Stepping into the foyer, I walked into the living room to find Marley, Olivia, and Penelope dancing around the room to I Love It by Icona Pop and Charli XCX.

"Oh, hey." Marley smiled, turning off the music.

"You three look like you're having fun." I walked over and kissed her lips.

"We were, McBillionaire." Olivia walked by and patted his chest. "We're going to go. Talk to you tomorrow." She hugged Marley.

"Yeah. See you tomorrow." Penelope hugged Marley. "Bye, Charlie."

"Good night, ladies." A smile crossed my lips. I grabbed the small remote, put on a slow song, placed my arm around Marley, and began dancing.

"Oh, are we having a dance, Mr. Stone?" She grinned.

"We are." I tenderly kissed her lips. "I got in touch with

a friend of mine from college. She's going to check into Troy for you."

"Really? Who is this friend of yours?"

"Her name is Morgan, and she's the best hacker there is. If there's anything to be found about Troy, she'll find it."

"Thank you for doing this for me." Her arms tightened around my neck. "I love you."

"I love you, too, babe. I told her all about you, and she wants to meet you. As soon as she finds out something about Troy, we'll have dinner together."

～

One Week Later

WHEN I HEARD the elevator coming up, I walked into the foyer. When the doors opened, Morgan stepped out, and I hugged her.

"Thanks for coming."

"I'm loving the new digs, Charlie." She grinned. "Wow."

"Thanks." I chuckled.

I led her into the kitchen, where Marley pulled the chicken from the oven.

"Marley, I'd like you to meet Morgan Ashley. Morgan, this is my beautiful girlfriend, Marley.

"It's so nice to meet you." Marley smiled, hugging her.

"It's nice to meet you, too, Marley. Wow. Look at you." Morgan smiled. "You are a very beautiful pregnant woman."

"You're sweet. Thank you."

"I have to admit that I was shocked when Charlie told me the two of you were having twins."

"Trust me. We both were." A smirk crossed Marley's lips.

The three of us sat down, talked, and ate the wonderful dinner Marley cooked for us. Afterward, I poured Morgan another glass of wine, and we got down to business.

"So, your boy, Troy Truman, is in some serious financial trouble with gambling debts, bad investments and call girls. He was fired from Chase Morgan last month because he was losing clients who were unhappy with their returns. He overpromised and underdelivered."

"But he was just on a two-week business trip," Marley said.

"That wasn't for his previous employer. That was for an investment that went wrong. I did some digging on your client, Allison. The day she marries, she inherits the trust fund her parents set up when she was born."

"That's why he's in such a rush to marry her," Marley said. "She mustn't know he was fired."

"Probably not. I found a passport application with his picture and a different name. My guess is that he'll talk her into investing her money, put it in an off-shore account, and disappear without a trace."

"Oh, my God. That poor girl. She is so sweet and trusts him completely. Wait a second. When we were looking at wedding invitations, she told me that he didn't want anyone from his work at the wedding, only family and a few close friends. How could I have slept with that disgusting pig?"

"It wasn't your fault, babe." I reached over and took hold of Marley's hand. "Just forget it ever happened."

"It happens to the best of us." Morgan smirked.

"I can't let her marry him," Marley said.

"I don't think you'll have to worry about that. I've sent Allison and her father some of his financial documents with an anonymous letter about his recent unemployment."

"They won't know where they came from, right?" I asked with worry.

"No. Have you forgotten who you're talking to?" Morgan's brow arched.

"Not at all." I chuckled.

"She's going to be heartbroken." Marley pouted.

"It's better she finds out now before marrying his broke, deceptive, cheating ass." A smile crossed Morgan's lips. "I wouldn't be surprised if you receive a call from the bride-to-be tonight."

After Morgan left, I helped Marley clean up from dinner. Her phone rang as we headed to the bedroom to get ready for bed.

"Charlie, it's Allison's mother." Her eyes widened.

"Answer it." We sat on the edge of the bed, and she put it on speaker.

"Hello."

"Marley, it's Adele."

"Hi, Adele."

"I don't know how to tell you this, but we will no longer be needing your services. Allison called off the wedding."

"Oh no, Adele. I'm so sorry."

"We're not. It turns out Troy isn't the man she thought he was. Could you please cancel everything for us?"

"Of course. I'll do that first thing tomorrow. Is Allison okay?"

"No, she isn't. She's heartbroken, but she'll be fine. I'm putting a check in the mail first thing tomorrow for your fee and some extra to compensate you for having to call the wedding off."

"Thank you, Adele. I appreciate it. Please give Allison my best."

"I will. Thank you, Marley."

She ended the call and lay her head on my shoulder as my arm wrapped around her.

"That poor girl," she said.

"She'll be fine, babe. Like Morgan said, it's better she found out now before he married her and ripped her off."

The following morning, as Marley and I stood in the kitchen, drinking a cup of coffee before I left for work, my phone rang.

"It's Morgan," I said, looking at Marley. "Good morning, Morgan." I put the call on speaker.

"Good morning, Charlie. I wanted to inform you that I got an alert that our boy, Troy, has skipped out of the country."

"Already?" I asked. "Allison's mother called Marley last night and told her the wedding was called off."

"That's good to hear. He wiped out his bank account and hopped on a plane to Switzerland. I'm not sure why he chose there, but he won't be in the States any time soon, if ever."

"Thanks, Morgan. I owe you one."

"You're welcome, Charlie. Hi, Marley!"

"Hi, Morgan. Thank you for everything."

"No problem. You two have a good day."

"You too, Morgan." I ended the call and slipped my phone into my pocket.

"I can't believe he went to Switzerland. What the hell is there?" Marley's brows furrowed.

"Who knows. Maybe he likes Swiss girls." I smirked. "You probably sent him over the edge when you told him the twins were his." I narrowed my eyes.

"I hope I did." She grinned, patting me on the chest.

"Don't give me that look. You know he deserved it and even more now. I love you. Go to work." She reached up and kissed my lips.

"Stay out of trouble while I'm gone." I bent down and kissed her large belly. "You two behave in there."

Chapter Twenty-Seven

MARLEY

"Are you ready to do this?" I glanced at Charlie as we stood hand in hand outside of Crate & Kids.

"I think so. Are you?"

"I'll let you know once we get in there."

He chuckled, opening the door, and we stepped inside.

"Okay. I'm overwhelmed," I said, looking at the cribs.

"This one is nice," Charlie said.

"Really?" I scrunched my nose. "It looks like a prison cell. Now, this one is beautiful." I ran my hand along the spindle wood crib.

"That one is nice. Do you want the same crib for both kids?" he asked.

"I think so. We can decorate one with pink bedding and the other in blue or gray."

He flipped over the price tag. "Damn. Fifteen hundred dollars for one crib?"

"Is that too expensive for your children?" I cocked my head. "I have an idea. How about we just buy a wooden box for them to sleep in? Maybe an extra large one for both of them to share."

"Are you finished?" His right eye narrowed.

"Maybe. Maybe not."

"The price doesn't matter to me one bit. I commented on it because it's just a crib they won't use very long."

"But the tag says it converts to a toddler bed, too," I said.

"Oh, in that case, I think fifteen hundred is a good price." He grinned.

"Hello. I'm Mara. Is there anything I can help you with?" The lovely sales associate smiled.

"We're just picking out furniture for our nursery," I said.

"Just so you know. Everything here has to be ordered, and it's about a six-to-eight-week delivery time. It looks like you're due very soon, so I just wanted to let you know. Most parents want the nursery done well before their baby is born."

I stood and listened to her with a smile, even though I was ready to claw her eyes out.

"That will be more than enough time. I'm pregnant with twins. Perhaps that is why you thought I'd be giving birth any day now."

"Oh. I'm so sorry. I just—"

"Thought I was giving birth to a giant?" I cocked my head, and Charlie placed his arm around me and squeezed me.

"It's fine." He smiled at Mara. "We would like to order two of these cribs, the dresser, chest, and glider."

"Two gliders." I smiled.

"Why do we need two of them?" he asked with furrowed brows.

"So I can rock one baby, and you can rock the other, silly."

"I don't think both gliders will fit in the room, babe."

"Then we'll have to knock down the wall between the bedrooms and turn it into one large one."

"Then the penthouse will only be a three-bedroom home. I think for resale value——"

"Then you shouldn't have made your office/game room so big," I pursed my lips.

"Right." He sighed. "Make it two gliders."

"Have you picked out the bassinets yet?" Mara asked.

"Why do we need those?" I asked. "We're buying the cribs."

"So your babies will be by you during the night. The bassinet is smaller, which creates a safer sleeping option for the newborn. Besides, it reduces the risk of sudden infant death syndrome. This one over here is our most popular."

Suddenly, anxiety began to creep inside me. Pulling out my phone, I sent a text to Penelope.

"Do I need to get bassinets for the babies?"

"I would. Everyone I know who has kids always has them. They're very convenient for the first few months."

"And who do you know who has kids?"

"All of my cousins do. Just get the damn bassinets, Mar."

"We'll take two of those." I smiled.

After leaving the store, we headed over to Babesta to look at other baby items.

"We're going to need a double stroller," I said.

"I figured as much," Charlie said.

"Oh, here's one. Look at how nice this is." I smiled. "Oh, it has a cup holder attachment for my coffee."

"Two thousand dollars? Seriously?" Charlie's brow arched.

"You're right. I'll just strap them to my back when I leave the penthouse."

"Babe, knock it off." He kissed the side of my head. "I guess I didn't realize how expensive baby things were."

"Well, you have no right to complain. Only one condom was used. Remember that." A smirk crossed my lips as I patted his chest.

CHARLIE

I was sitting behind my desk when my phone rang. Glancing at it, I saw Miles Bradshaw was calling.

"Miles, how are you, my friend?"

"I'm great, Charlie. How are you?"

"No complaints. What can I do for you?"

"Listen, I know you practically just moved into the penthouse, but I wanted to let you know that the town-home next door to me just went up for sale. I figured with the twins coming, you might want something a little bigger. George and Micah just remodeled the entire home and have decided to move to Hawaii, where their daughter and son-in-law are. I guess she's pregnant with their first child. It's a beautiful home, Charlie, and trust me when I tell you, with two babies coming at once, you'll need all the room you can get."

Leaning back in my chair, I sighed. "I was thinking about that ever since Marley and I were at the baby store buying all the furniture and equipment for the twins. I just called my contractor this morning because Marley wants to knock out one of the walls of two bedrooms and make it one large room. Thanks for letting me know. I'll give Grant a call."

"You're welcome, Charlie. I'll talk to you later."

Dialing Grant, he answered on the first ring.

"Charlie, my friend. What can I do for you?"

"Hey, Grant. Miles Bradshaw just called and told me the townhome next door to him is for sale."

"Yeah, it is. It went up yesterday."

"I would like to see it."

"Seriously? You're thinking about moving already?" he asked.

"It's just a thought. When can I see it?"

"I'm over that way now at another showing. Can you be at the house in half an hour?"

"You bet. I'll see you then."

I texted Mateo to get the car ready. I grabbed my suit-coat, and Chase walked in as I was heading out of my office.

"Where are you going?" he asked.

"To look at a townhome."

"What?" He chuckled. "You want to move again?"

"It's not that I want to, but I think it's what's best for us."

"You better have that awesome gaming room in the new place." A smirk crossed his lips.

"You know I will." I grinned.

As I climbed out of the car at the curb, I saw Stella leaving her house with her nanny and the kids.

"Charlie? How are you?"

"I'm good, Stella." I hugged her.

"What are you doing here?"

"Your husband called earlier and told me the house next door is for sale. I'm meeting Grant." I looked at my watch. "He should be here any second."

"Oh, I hope you love it! It's a beautiful home. I couldn't ask for better neighbors than you and Marley." She grinned.

Grant's car pulled up, and he climbed out.

"Good luck, Charlie." Stella smiled.

"Let me show you this gorgeous home, my friend." Grant patted my back.

After unlocking the door, I stepped inside.

"Wow," I spoke, placing my hands in my pants pockets as I toured the place. "It's practically brand new. Adalyn did this, right? I know her work anywhere." I smiled.

"She did. Isn't it beautiful? I don't expect it to be on the market long. The owners haven't lived here in over six months. They went to their Hawaii home to stay while it was being remodeled. Their daughter found out she was pregnant, and they decided to stay there permanently. They came back last week to get the rest of their clothes and personal items. The movers just moved everything out a few days ago. It's a great neighborhood with excellent schools. And there's a lot to be said about your neighbors." He grinned.

"I really like this house. What about my penthouse? I don't want to take a loss."

"If you want my opinion, I'd rent it out for a couple of years with the option to buy. In fact, Bella may have a couple who would be interested in renting it. Just let me know."

"I'll go home and talk to Marley about it and call you in the morning. She's going to want to see it first."

"I can be here first thing tomorrow before heading to the office," he said.

"Thank you, my friend." I smiled, extending my hand.

"You're welcome, Charlie."

Chapter Twenty-Eight

MARLEY

I was standing in the middle of the bedroom that we would convert into a nursery, trying to picture where all the furniture would go once the wall came down.

"There you are." Charlie grinned as he walked over and kissed me. "What are you doing in here?"

"Trying to mentally place all the furniture we bought. I was thinking that the cribs—"

"Come with me." Charlie grabbed my hand and led me out of the room.

"Excuse me. I was trying to tell you something." My brows furrowed as he led me over to the couch.

"Sit back and bring your legs on my lap. There's something I want to discuss with you."

I sat on the couch, and he rubbed my aching feet.

"Oh my God," I moaned. "You're totally forgiven."

He let out a chuckle. "Miles Bradshaw called me today. The townhome next to his and Stella's is up for sale. I went and looked at it today."

"A townhome? You want to move?" I asked. "You just bought this place."

"I know, and I'm not worried about that. We need a bigger place for us and the kids."

"How big are we talking?" I arched my brow.

"This particular home is eight thousand square feet with six bedrooms and eight bathrooms."

"Who needs eight bathrooms, Charlie?"

"Babe, they come with the house. Anyway, Grant said he'd show it to us tomorrow morning. I really like it and want your thoughts. The home has been completely remodeled and is ready to be moved into. The owners are living in Hawaii."

"But what about your gaming room? You love that space."

"And I'll put another one in the new house." He winked.

"But this is your ultimate bachelor pad, Charlie."

"You're my girlfriend who is having my two children. I don't think I'm a bachelor anymore who needs the ultimate bachelor pad. What do you say? Do you want to see it?"

"Yes. Of course, I do."

"Good. I'll call Grant and tell him."

"After you rub my feet some more." I smiled.

"Anything you say, sweetheart." A smile crossed his lips.

"I think I'll reward you after dinner. My entire body may ache, but my mouth doesn't."

"Fuck dinner." He pushed my legs off him, stood up, and picked me up from the couch. "Oh, God. I hate to say it, but I think this may be the last time I can pick you up." He carried me to the bedroom.

"IT'S PERFECT, CHARLIE." I covered my mouth with my hand in awe of the home.

"The only thing we'll need to do are the nurseries."

"What do you mean?" I cocked my head. "We can't separate the twins right now. Once they get older, yes. But for now, we need one big nursery."

"Let's go take a look." He grabbed my hand and led me to the fourth floor.

"What's the point of this small ass room?" I asked. "No. You're going to have to knock this wall down and make this room bigger. This will be the twin's room for now, and then, when they get older, we'll put one of them across the hall in that big room."

"You seriously want to knock down this wall?"

"Yep. Get rid of it." I waved my hand. "It's a useless room, Charlie. You'll barely get a twin bed and dresser in there."

"I see your point." He sighed, rubbing the back of his neck. "I'll call the contractor."

"Perfect." I grinned. "Then your gaming room/office can be one floor up." I kissed his cheek. "Have I told you how in love I am with you?"

"You have, babe. I love you too."

"We'll take it, Grant!" I beamed with excitement.

"Excellent. I know the four of you will be very happy here." He grinned. "I'll draw up the contract, Charlie, and call you when it's ready. By the way, Bella spoke to her client, and they are excited to see the penthouse. They're flying in tomorrow from Los Angeles. I'll have Bella call you to set up a time for them to come look at it."

"Thank you, Grant." Charlie shook his hand.

When we walked out of the house, I saw Stella and Melissa taking the kids from the car.

"Well?" Stella smiled from the curb.

"Howdy, neighbor!" I waved with a wide grin.

"EEK!" She ran over and hugged me. "Ah, I'm so happy you two bought the place. Miles will be excited, too!"

After saying goodbye to Stella, Charlie and I climbed into the back of the car.

"Mateo, can you drop me off at Love At First Sip?"

"Of course, Marley."

"I'm excited to tell Penelope and Olivia." I smiled, glancing at Charlie.

"I bet you are." He leaned over and kissed me.

I walked into Love At First Sip with a smile.

"Why did you reject our Facetime call this morning?" Olivia asked.

"And why did you turn off your location?" Penelope's eyes narrowed.

"I didn't. Check?" I smiled.

They both pulled out their phones. "I call bullshit. You just turned it back on. What's going on?" Olivia said. "You know you can't lie to us."

"Come sit down." I grabbed their hands and pulled them with me to a table. "Charlie and I are moving to an eight thousand square foot townhome."

"Shut up!" Penelope exclaimed.

"Go McBillionaire." Olivia grinned. "I can't believe he's giving up his almighty bachelor pad."

"He says he's not a bachelor anymore since he has a girlfriend and two babies on the way. I can't wait for you to see it. It's huge. It's gorgeous." The smile on my face dissipated.

"Mar, what's wrong?" Penelope asked, grabbing my hand.

"It's too good to be true. He's too good to be true. Fuck my life." I placed my hand on my forehead.

"She's waiting for the shoe to drop," Olivia said.

"I think you're right," Penelope spoke. "Marley, you need to go talk to someone."

"No, I don't. I'm fine."

"Clearly, you're not, and you haven't been since you were eleven years old. Sorry, girl. But it's the damn truth."

"I love you guys, but I have to go." I stood up and walked out of the coffee shop.

Chapter Twenty-Nine

CHARLIE

"This is one of our finest diamonds," Ricardo spoke as he handed me the four-carat ring.

"Damn, Charlie. That ring is beautiful," Chase said.

"I'll take it, Ricardo." I handed him my credit card.

"Excellent. I'll be right back." A smile crossed his lips as he walked out of the room.

"When are you going to propose?" Chase asked.

"Soon. I want to do it before the twins are born."

"Look at you." He grinned, placing his hand on my shoulder. "My boy is all grown up, having babies, getting married."

"Knock it off." I chuckled.

"I never thought this day would come. I'm still in shock. Um, you did remember to turn your location off, right? You don't want Marley seeing you're at Cartier."

"Yes. I turned it off."

When Ricardo returned, I slipped the ring box into my pocket, and Chase and I left the store.

When I arrived home, the smell of Chinese food infiltrated the space.

"You ordered dinner?" I asked, walking into the kitchen, where Marley was already eating.

"Yeah. Sorry. I couldn't wait for you. The babies were starving. I hope you're in the mood for Chinese."

"Did you order the entire menu?" I chuckled, looking at all the cartons sitting on the table. Walking over to her, I kissed her lips.

"I couldn't decide, and everything sounded so good. Grab a plate and eat with me."

"Let me change first, and I'll join you."

Walking into the bedroom, I tucked the ring box into one of my drawers for safekeeping until I figured out a plan. After changing my clothes, I returned to the kitchen, grabbed a bottle of water from the refrigerator, and sat at the table.

"I saw on Facebook today that a couple who hired me a year ago to plan their wedding are getting divorced," Marley said, shoving a forkful of food in her mouth.

"Oh yeah?"

"Yep. This is why people shouldn't get married. The goal of a relationship is to stay together. Marriage doesn't guarantee that so why bother spending all that time and money trying to prove to the world that you will make it as a couple? If two people are madly in love with each other, they don't need a piece of paper to confirm it."

I stared blankly at her from across the table, not believing what I heard.

"What?" she asked.

"I didn't know you felt that way about marriage. I mean, you do plan weddings."

"It's my job." She cocked her head. "Besides, don't you agree?"

"I don't know if I do or don't. My parents were happily married. Don't you think you're basing your decision because of your parents?"

"Probably." She wiped her mouth with a napkin, grabbed her plate, and walked over to the sink. "But the divorce rate is so high. People just rush into it because they like the concept of a wedding, the fairytale of it all, and think they'll get their happily-ever-after once they say, 'I do.' That piece of paper only complicates things."

I was getting angrier by the second. Throwing my napkin down, I stood up and walked out of the kitchen.

"Charlie?"

I went to the bedroom and sat on the edge of the bed.

"What's wrong?" Marley asked, walking into the room.

"All this talk about marriage," I said.

"I know, right? I'm sorry I went on a rant." She sat down and softly rubbed my back. "Oh!" She grabbed my hand and placed it on her belly. "The babies are kicking." She smiled.

I felt the little flutters against my hand. "They sure are." I leaned in and kissed the side of her head. "We haven't discussed names for them yet."

"I know. We should do that." She brought her hand up to my face and softly stroked it.

Not too long ago, I didn't want marriage or children. But I'd come to realize that I was wrong because the right woman never walked into my life. Now that I had the right woman and she was having my babies, everything changed. I wanted the entire package.

The following morning, I sat behind my desk and stared out the window at the busy city.

"Morning." I heard Chase's cheerful voice.

"Morning." I turned my chair around.

"You look tired. What's wrong?"

"I was up all night." I sighed.

"Ah, having great sex with your soon-to-be fiancée?"

"We had sex, but she's not my soon-to-be fiancée."

"What are you talking about?" His brows furrowed.

"Marley brought up marriage last night and went on a rant about how she doesn't believe in it."

"Oh shit, Charlie. You didn't tell her you were going to propose, did you?"

"No way. You should have heard her, Chase."

"What are you going to do?"

"I guess just keep calling her my girlfriend for the rest of my life. What the hell can I do? She wants nothing to do with marriage."

"Some people are like that, I guess. It doesn't mean she doesn't love you."

"I know she loves me, but I don't want to be unmarried for the rest of my life. I want that final commitment."

"Damn, listen to you." A smile crossed his lips. "Not too long ago, you were saying the exact opposite."

"That was before I met Marley. I love her and want to make her my wife."

"Listen, Charlie. When the time is right, she'll change her mind, and it'll happen. Right now, she's just flooded with hormones and very pregnant. Anyway, I just stopped in to say good morning. I'm headed to a meeting with the staff. I'll see you later."

Chapter Thirty

TWO WEEKS LATER

MARLEY

The movers were packing boxes and getting ready to move us out of the penthouse. I was excited and exhausted at the same time. Penelope and Olivia were over, helping me go through some of my clothes in the bedroom.

"Do either of you want this dress? I'll never wear it again." I held the dress up in front of them.

"I do!" Penelope grinned. "I always loved that dress."

One of the movers opened one of Charlie's drawers to pack his clothes, and we heard something fall on the floor.

"What's this?" Olivia walked over and picked up what looked like a ring box. "Holy shit!" She exclaimed.

Walking over to her, I placed my hand over my mouth as I stared at the large, flawless diamond.

"I wonder how long he's had this," Penelope said, staring at the ring.

Anxiety started to infiltrate me as I told the mover to put all of Charlie's T-shirts back in the drawer and leave the room. I did what I always did best: I started to hyperventilate.

"Mar, calm the fuck down." Olivia grabbed my hand and led me to the bed.

"Slow, deep breaths." Penelope gripped my shoulders, her face mere inches from mine.

I couldn't believe Charlie had bought me an engagement ring.

"You have to marry him when he asks you," Olivia said. "I know you're fucked up, but this is a time when you need to un-fuck yourself and accept the fact that McBillionaire loves you and those babies more than anything else."

I lay down on my back and stared up at the ceiling. My breathing returned to normal, but my heart was still racing.

"I can't deal with this right now. There's too much to do. Put it back in the drawer."

"Mar—" Penelope said.

"I said put it back in the drawer!"

"Okay. Okay." Olivia stood up, walked over to the drawer, and placed the box inside.

Later that evening, when Charlie arrived home, I greeted him with a kiss.

"Hello there." He smiled.

"I missed you." I tightened my arms around his neck.

"I missed you too. Did the movers get the bedroom packed up?"

"Everything but what's in the dresser drawers," I said.

"Why?"

"I told them we'd do it. I don't want strangers packing my underwear and nighties. Do you?" I arched my brow.

"I don't really care, babe. But that's fine. I can pack my drawers."

"I already did mine. I can't believe we're moving tomorrow."

"I know. Me either." He pulled me into him.

One Month Later

"LOOK AT THOSE LITTLE SNUG BUGS." Dr. Gregario grinned. "Baby A and Baby B are doing just fine."

Charlie and I stared at our babies on the monitor with smiles.

"I can't believe how much they've grown," Charlie said.

"Oh, I can. I feel it every day."

"Okay, Marley. We have you on the schedule for a C-section next month. I'll see you next week. If you have any questions or concerns, call me."

"Thank you, Dr. Gregario."

"I don't think I can go another month," I pouted, staring at Charlie.

"You can do it, babe." He kissed my forehead and helped me up from the table.

"How do you know that? Because I know for a fact that you wouldn't be able to carry two human beings inside you."

"You're right." He hooked his arm around me as we left the office. "But you're going to get through it for the sake of our son and daughter."

"I guess you're right." I sighed as he opened the car door, and I slid inside.

It had been a month since I'd found the ring he'd bought me. Every time we went to dinner, or he planned something special, anxiety took over because I thought that was the night he'd pop the question. I kept waiting, but he never asked. I started to remember the night I told him about the couple I planned the wedding for getting a divorce and everything I spewed about marriage. He must have had the ring because I remembered him getting up from the table and walking away. Fuck. I ruined it for him. And all because of how fucked up I was, thanks to my mother.

After dropping Charlie back at the office, Mateo drove me home—our new home, which we spent the last month decorating with new furniture, décor, and the nursery.

When I stepped inside, the clean, fresh smell from Greta's cleaning greeted me. Setting my purse down, I grabbed my phone, went upstairs, and sat in the rocker in the nursery with my hand on my belly, rocking back and forth. Dialing my mother, she answered.

"Marley, this is a nice surprise."

"Hey, Mom. How are you?"

"I'm good. Have the babies arrived?"

"No." I let out a soft laugh. "I was wondering if you're going to be home tomorrow. I was going to stop by."

"Yes, honey. I'll be home."

"Great. I'll be over around eleven."

"Great. I can't wait to see you. It's been a while."

"Yeah. It has. I'll see you tomorrow."

I ended the call and closed my eyes for a moment. I had this crazy craving for Taco Bell and couldn't shake it.

"Hey, beautiful," Charlie answered when I called.

"Hi, handsome. I just called to let you know that I'm craving Taco Bell in a crazy way."

"I see. When I get home, how about we go to that Mexican restaurant we like?"

"The babies are specifically craving Taco Bell, Charlie."

"Okay. Taco Bell it is." He chuckled. "Text me what you want. I'll be home in a couple of hours."

"Thanks. I love you."

"I love you too, babe. I'll see you soon."

CHARLIE

"Taco Bell?" Chase's brow arched. "Nasty."

"It's what she and babies want." I smiled.

"I meant to ask you. Did you ever take the ring you bought back?"

"No. It's still buried in my drawer. Maybe one day she'll change her mind."

"I can tell it's been bothering you," Chase said.

"I try not to think about it. Things are great with us, and the twins will be here soon. If she doesn't want to get married, I need to respect that."

"But you never asked her, Charlie. You don't know for sure that she'd say no."

"You didn't hear her that night, and honestly, I think her rejection would be worse. I'm grateful for what we have, and I'm not pushing it. Let's talk about that new game we want to develop."

After leaving the office, I had Mateo drop me off at the Mexican restaurant to pick up a carry-out order before stopping at Taco Bell. I wasn't about to eat that crap, and I knew once Marley smelled the food from the place we loved, she'd dump the Taco Bell.

Stepping through the front door, I headed to the kitchen and set the bags of food on the island.

"I thought I heard you come in." Marley smiled, walking into the kitchen.

"It feels good to be home." I gripped her hips and kissed her.

"What's this?" She pointed to the bag from the other restaurant.

"I stopped and got that for me. Go take your Taco Bell and sit down." A smirk crossed my lips as I handed her the bag.

We sat down at the table, and I noticed her staring at me as she bit into her burrito supreme.

"What?" I smiled.

"Nothing." She continued to stare.

"This is so good. This restaurant never fails to serve the best Mexican," I said.

"Yeah. They do have really good food." She took another bite of her burrito and set it down. "What?" She placed her hand on her belly and looked down. "You two want what Daddy's having? But he stopped and got this great Taco Bell for us."

"Marley, would you like some?" I held out my fork to her.

"Yes!" She grabbed it and stuck it in her mouth. "Oh, my God. This is so good. You know it's my favorite."

I stood up, walked over to the island, and removed her food from the bag.

"Here." I smiled, setting the food in front of her. "I knew you'd change your mind about the Taco Bell."

"God, I love you. Thank you."

"You're welcome." I chuckled, pressing my lips against the top of her head.

"I'm going to visit my mom tomorrow," she said.

"Oh yeah? How come?"

"It's been a while. I figured I better see her before the twins arrive."

"I'm sure she's happy you're coming. Be nice." I pointed my fork at her.

"Excuse me? I'm always nice. Can we play a video game together after we eat?"

"Music to my ears, baby." I winked.

Chapter Thirty-One

MARLEY

I walked up the steps to the front door of my childhood home and took in a long breath. This talk was years in the making, and I wasn't sure if I was ready.

"Marley, honey." My mom smiled, hugging me. "Goodness, look at that belly." She placed her hands on it. "I still can't believe you're having twins."

"Me either."

"Would you like some tea?" she asked as I followed her into the kitchen.

"Yeah. That would be great." I sat at the table. "We need to talk, Mom."

"About what?"

"About how messed up I am because of my childhood and what happened."

"We already talked about that years ago, Marley."

"No, Mom. You told me things happen in life we can't control. I need to know why you did it."

She set the teacups on the table and sat across from me.

"When Peter and Miranda moved in next door, I felt this instant connection to him—a connection I'd never felt with anyone before. It scared me. After years of trying to deny it, I couldn't anymore. I loved your father but wasn't in love with him. Honestly, I'm not sure I ever was."

"Then why did you marry him?" I asked.

"I was going through a rough time. Your grandmother was very ill, and he was there for me through it all, even after she passed away. He was the comfort I needed at the time. One afternoon, my friend Linda and I took you and went shopping. A new cute little shop had opened up. It was a shop that sold crystals and different metaphysical items. The owner, Hallie, had different classes you could take, and she offered psychic services. Linda thought it would be fun to get readings, so we made an appointment, went back, and had them done. Hallie told me that I had met my soulmate, but it wasn't your father. I knew right then she was talking about Peter. You have to understand, Marley, that I was unhappy."

"Then why didn't you just divorce Dad first?"

"I don't know. I guess I was trying to protect you."

"Protect me? Do you have any idea what that did to me, seeing you in bed with him at eleven years old? And then telling me to lie to Dad about it?"

"I was wrong, and I've apologized to you for that already. I know I've ruined our relationship because you never forgave me."

"Maybe it's time I did forgive you because the twins will need their grandmother."

"Marley." Tears filled her eyes.

We talked a while longer, hugged each other, and then I left. Instead of driving back to Manhattan, I decided to do some shopping in Long Island. It had been a long time since I explored some of the stores. I stopped into a baby store and picked up a few sleepers for the twins. I already had so many, but these were so cute I couldn't resist. Walking down the street, I passed the crystal shop my mother talked about. I stopped, turned around, and stepped inside. I'd passed this store a thousand times and never went in.

I looked around at the different items. An older woman emerged from the back and greeted me.

"Good afternoon. Oh my, twins." She smiled.

"Yes. I am having twins." I placed my hand on my belly.

"One of each—a boy and a girl. Congratulations."

"And what if I didn't know the sex of the twins?" I arched my brow.

"You already know." She smiled.

"Hallie, right?"

"Yes." She cocked her head.

"My mother told me about you. She had a reading done years ago. I was just visiting her and doing some shopping and thought I'd stop in."

Her brows furrowed, and she took hold of my hand, sandwiching it between hers.

"You have a beautiful soul among all the turmoil that consumed your life."

"How do you know about the turmoil in my life?"

"I see it in your soul. I can feel it as I hold your hand."

This woman was freaking me out. I pulled my hand out of hers.

"Thank you for telling me I have a beautiful soul. I have to get back to the city." I turned and headed toward the door.

"Marley?"

I stopped dead in my tracks and turned around. How the hell did she know my name?

"You have nothing to fear. You've found your soulmate. It was decided the day the two of you met. It's time to let go of the past and create the life you were destined to live."

I gave her a small smile and left the shop. Climbing into my car, I gripped the steering wheel. My phone rang, and when I pulled it from my purse, I saw Charlie was calling.

"Hey. I was just thinking about you," I said.

"Hello, beautiful. I was thinking about you, too. Are you doing some shopping with your mom?"

"How do you know I'm shopping?"

"I may have been stalking your location."

"I did do some shopping, but not with my mom." I pulled away from the curb.

"Did things not go well with her?" he asked.

"Things went fine. We had a nice talk. After I left, I wanted to do some shopping alone."

"Are you okay?"

"I'm good, Charlie. I'm heading home now."

"Judging by your location, you just left. Sit tight, and I'll send Mateo to come get you. You're going to hit major traffic on the way back at this time."

"I'm not sitting around waiting for Mateo. I do know how to drive."

"I'm sure you do, and it's not you I'm worried about. It's the assholes on the road."

"I need you to stop worrying so much. Keep my location open and watch my little car drive home. It'll make you feel better."

"Good idea. I'll do it now, babe."

"I know you will. I love you. I have to concentrate on the road now."

"I love you too. Drive safe, and I'll see you when I get home."

His worrying annoyed me at times but made me smile. I was jamming to the radio and feeling exhausted from the drive. I was thirty minutes from being home, and I couldn't wait to lie down. My lower back had been killing me all day, something fierce, and I needed my sexy boyfriend to massage it. At least I had some entertainment. The couple in the car in front of me were arguing. He was yelling and throwing his hands up. She was yelling back and pointing at him. It was quite humorous until he suddenly slammed on the brakes, and my car rammed into his back end. I froze, gripping the steering wheel. The airbag didn't go off, thank God, because we weren't going that fast, and I didn't hit hard—just enough to shake me up. Oh, shit. How was I going to tell Charlie?

The man climbed out of the car. He was angry and headed toward me.

"Oh, no, asshole. You don't get to be mad," I mumbled, climbing out of the car.

He stopped when he saw me, taking note of my oversized belly.

"Oh, my God!" The woman in the passenger seat ran over to me. "Are you okay?"

"I think so."

"Look at what you did, asshole!" she yelled at the man. "All because you don't know how to control your anger!"

"Ma'am, I'm sorry," The man spoke.

"Why the hell did you slam on your brakes?" I shouted, placing my hand on my lower back. "There wasn't anyone in front of you!"

"She pissed me off." He pointed at the girl.

"Oh yeah, dickhead. Blame me!" she shouted back.

"We need to call the police," I said, reaching inside my car and grabbing my phone.

"No. Don't," the guy said. "I'll give you my name and number. Please, lady. No cops."

"Sorry, but we need to file a police report," I said, dialing 911.

"Yasmin, get the fuck in the car!" the man shouted.

"Oh, hell no! Don't you dare!" I ran after the man.

It was too late. He and his woman climbed into the car and locked the doors. Thank God I had enough sense to take a picture of the license plate number before he could get away. My phone rang, and it was Charlie. Shit.

"Hello."

"What happened? Why did you suddenly stop?"

"Charlie, take a deep breath."

"Marley, what the hell happened?"

"I was in a little fender bender." I bit my bottom lip.

"WHAT?!" he shouted. "I'm on my way. Did you call the police?"

"I'm trying to, but you're keeping me from doing it!"

"The other person didn't call?" he asked.

"He took off."

"WHAT? Call 911 right now and stay out of harm's way. I'm on my way now." He abruptly ended the call.

"Goodbye to you too." I sighed.

I dialed 911, and two police officers arrived. Ten minutes after the officers got there, Charlie pulled up.

"Are you okay?" He grabbed and hugged me tight.

"I'm fine."

"Miss Monroe, you said you got the license plate number?" the officer asked.

"Yes." I brought up the picture on my phone.

"That's good." He wrote the number down. "Do you need medical attention?"

"No. I'm fine. I just want to go home," I said.

"You're going to the hospital," Charlie said.

"Stop." I placed my hand on his chest. "The airbag didn't go off, and I didn't hit him that hard. I'm fine."

"That's it. I knew I shouldn't have let you drive to Long Island. I'm buying another car and hiring you your own driver."

I wouldn't lie; I loved the idea.

"Whatever you say. I want to go home."

He hooked his arm around me and pulled me into him as we walked to his car. The pain in my lower back was getting worse, and suddenly, an intense cramping in my belly gripped me.

"OH GOD!" I doubled over.

"Marley, what's wrong?" Charlie asked, holding me against him.

"I think we should go to the hospital." I looked at him with worry.

He slowly led me to where Mateo was parked down the street and opened the door. I climbed inside and tried to keep calm. The pain subsided, and fear tore through me.

"What if the accident did something to the babies?" Tears filled my eyes.

"Don't, Marley. You and the twins are going to be okay. I promise." He pulled me into him and kissed my head.

A few moments later, the pain hit me again, and I let out a scream.

"Oh God. Charlie, I think I'm in labor. What the fuck? I have a C-section scheduled, so I don't experience labor. Call Olivia and Penelope and tell them we're on our way to the hospital."

Chapter Thirty-Two

CHARLIE

I was scared shitless, and I swore that the guy who caused the accident and took off would pay dearly.

Mateo pulled up to the ER. Climbing out, I ran inside and told the security guard that Marley was in labor. He grabbed a wheelchair, and I helped Marley get into it. A nurse ran over and immediately took us to the Labor and Delivery Unit.

"She was in a car accident about two hours ago," I told the nurse.

"It was just a minor one," Marley said.

I looked at her and shook my head. She was taken straight to a room and told to change into a gown.

"OH GOD!" She screamed. "Make it stop!"

"Hello. I'm Pepper, your nurse. My, you are handsome." She smiled at me. "Okay, Marley. By the way, love the name. Let's get you hooked up to the fetal monitor. You said you were in a car accident recently."

"Yes, she was. Just a couple of hours ago."

"When did the pain start?" Pepper asked.

"Well, I've had serious back pain all day."

"You have?" I cocked my head. "You didn't tell me that."

"I didn't think much of it, Charlie. Anyway, the actual gut-wrenching, stops your breathing, and makes you want to end it all pain started not too long after the accident."

"It sounds like to me that you've been laboring all day, and now it's progressing. I'll grab the ultrasound machine and Dr. Gregario will be in shortly."

"He's already here?" I asked.

"Yep. He just delivered a baby about thirty minutes ago." Pepper grinned.

I grabbed Marley's hand and pressed my lips against her forehead.

"Charlie, it's too soon for the baby's to be born. I'm so scared."

"Shh. Everything is going to be okay." I gripped her hand.

"What's this I hear about a car accident, young lady?" Dr. Gregario entered the room.

"It was minor, Dr. Gregario," Marley said.

The door opened, and Pepper walked in with the ultrasound machine.

"Let's see what's going on with the snug bugs."

He moved the transducer over Marley's belly, and my children appeared.

"The twins have finished baking and are ready to come out of the oven." Dr. Gregario grinned.

"But it's too soon," Marley said.

"Maybe by a week. But I'm confident they're going to be just fine. Are you ready to have your babies?"

"If you mean by C-section, yes. So, let's get moving here, doctor."

He chuckled. "I'll get the team in here to get you

prepped. Pepper, call the O.R. and tell them Twins A and B Stone are on their way."

"Yay!" Pepper clapped with excitement.

"Charlie, I think I'm going to have a panic attack."

"Look at me, babe. Remember the first time we met?" I smiled. "Remember how you waved your first-class ticket in my face?"

"Yes, I remember," she softly spoke.

"I knew right then I was in trouble."

"Why?"

"Because I felt something."

"You were annoyed." A light smile crossed her lips.

"I was infatuated." I kissed her forehead.

"Are you ready, Marley?" Pepper asked. "They're here to take you to the O.R."

"I'll be right behind you, babe." I held her hand as they wheeled her out of the room.

"I got you a pair of scrubs to change into," Pepper said, handing them to me. "You'll be more comfortable than in that fancy suit. Go change in the bathroom, and I'll take you to the O.R."

I went into the bathroom and changed into the scrubs. When I walked into the room, Penelope and Olivia were standing there.

"Damn." Olivia's eyes raked over me. "You'd make a fine doctor."

"Where is Marley?" Penelope asked.

"They're prepping her in the O.R. I have to get down there. Can one of you do me a favor and call her mom and dad?"

"I'll call her dad." Penelope smiled.

"And I'll call her mom," Olivia sighed.

"Thanks. I'll keep you both updated." I left the room with Pepper, and she took me to Marley.

The moment I stepped into the O.R., Marley looked at me and held out her hand. Gripping it, I sat on the stool next to her.

"Hi." I smiled.

"Hi. Guess what?"

"What?" I asked.

"I feel no pain." She grinned.

"That's great, babe."

Dr. Gregario walked into the O.R. and took his place.

"Let's deliver these babies, shall we?"

"I love you so much." I held her hand.

"I love you more."

"Here comes Baby A," Dr. Gregario said, holding up our baby girl.

The sound of her cries was the sweetest thing I'd ever heard.

"Is she okay?" Marley asked.

"She's pure perfection, Marley," Dr. Gregario said.

A few moments later, our son was born, and his cry was stronger than his sister's. Tears streamed down my face when I saw my children for the first time.

"Welcome to the world Ashley and Ashton Stone."

MARLEY

I was a mom, and I couldn't believe it. When I stared at my babies, everything that had ever gone wrong in my life was now right. I was exhausted, and the four day stay in the hospital was welcomed, but I was more than ready to go home.

Penelope and Olivia came to the hospital the morning I was being discharged to help gather the flowers and gifts that our friends and family sent. Charlie and I dressed the twins in their 'going home' outfits, took multiple pictures, and set them in their car seats. As I was wheeled down to the lobby, Charlie was in front of me, holding the car seats in each hand. I held up my phone and took a video.

"There is nothing sexier than a man carrying his two children out of the hospital," Olivia said.

"He's one fine daddy," Penelope spoke. "Damn."

"He sure is." I grinned.

Chapter Thirty-Three

TWO WEEKS LATER

CHARLIE

I knew having twins wasn't going to be a walk in the park, but for fuck's sake, I had no idea it would be as hard as it was. Even though Marley and I thought we were prepared, we weren't.

"I know you said we'd hold off on a nanny until the twins were a little older, but we need to do something," I said, pacing around the room, trying to soothe Ashton.

"I feel like I'm going crazy, Charlie. Please check me into a mental institution. I'm begging you."

"Oh no. You're not getting off that easy."

There was a knock on the door, and when I walked over and opened it, Stella stood there with a smile.

"How's parenthood going?"

"Difficult. Come on in." I chuckled.

"Here, let me take him."

I handed Ashton over to Stella. She held him in a certain position, and he immediately quieted down.

"How did you do that?" I asked.

"I used to be a nanny, remember?" She smirked. "Actually, that's why I'm here."

"You're going to be our nanny?" Marley grinned.

"I know someone who would be perfect for you," she said. "Her name is Tilly, and she has a lot of experience with twins. The family she nannied for just moved to Chicago, so she's looking for another family. You'll love her."

"Send her over ASAP," I said. "I have to return to the office in a couple of days."

"I knew you'd say that, so I already told her about you. I can call and have her come over today if you want."

Stella called Tilly and set up an interview for four o'clock. After we thanked her and she lay Ashton in his bassinet, she went home. Walking over to the couch, I sat next to Marley and hooked my arm around her as Ashley slept peacefully in her arms.

"She's so beautiful." I smiled, staring at my daughter.

"When she's like this, yes, she is." Marley smirked.

"We'll get through this, babe." I kissed the side of her head.

"Do you really think so?"

"I know so. We have three hours before Tilly gets here. Let's go lay this little one in her bassinet and take a nap." I carefully took Ashley from Marley's arms and set her in the bassinet by her brother. Grabbing a blanket from the basket in the corner of the room, I sat back on the couch, covered us with the blanket, and hooked my arm around Marley. "There. Now close your eyes."

"You are truly amazing," she whispered.

"So are you, babe." I closed my eyes.

The earth-shattering screams of both children woke us from a deep sleep. Glancing at my watch, we'd only been sleeping a half hour.

"Oh, come on," Marley said.

"I'll get Ashley, and you get Ashton," I sighed, getting up from the couch.

∽

Two Weeks Later

MARLEY

I cleaned up from dinner while Charlie took the twins upstairs. It was hard to believe they were already a month old. We had survived the first month, and I was proud of us. Walking up to the bedroom, I stood in the doorway and watched Charlie with the twins on the bed. He was an incredible man and father. He took care of me. He got up every single night without one complaint. He changed diapers, fed them, played with them, and held them non-stop, even when I told him he was spoiling them. He held and comforted me when I was over-whelmed, hormonal, and sobbing. I never thought I could love anyone as much as I loved him. This man, Charlie Stone, was my life, and I couldn't imagine it without him.

I never really had the chance to process what Hallie told me that day in her shop because the accident happened, and the twins were born. Then, the chaos started when we brought them home, leaving us exhausted and unable to think clearly. His birthday was in a few days, and I wanted to plan something special for him and give him the ultimate gift.

∽

"HAVE you decided what you're giving Daddy

McBillionaire for a birthday gift?" Olivia asked as she held Ashley.

"I have." I grinned.

"Well, spit it out," Penelope said. "What do you give a billionaire who already has everything anyway?"

"A wife."

"Excuse me?" Olivia's brow arched.

"I'm going to ask Charlie to marry me. It's my fault that he never got to ask me, so I'm asking him."

"Yay!" Penelope grinned, clapping her hands.

"I'm proud of you, girl. Did you hear that, Ashley? Your mommy has finally grown up and come to her senses. She might not fuck you or your brother up after all." She lifted her and kissed her head.

"Very funny." My brows furrowed.

I WANTED to whisk Charlie away somewhere warm and romantic for his birthday, but I couldn't because the twins were only a month old. So, I decided to rent the Manhattan suite at the Lowell Hotel for the afternoon and night. Charlie hadn't a clue what my plans were and about the surprise birthday party Chase and Lila were throwing him at Chase's penthouse tomorrow night.

After giving Charlie his birthday present before he left for the office, I went upstairs while Tilly watched the twins and packed us each a bag. I was grateful to Penelope and Olivia for coming over later and spending the night with Tilly to help her with the babies.

I had everything planned, right down to the second I arrived at Charlie's office to whisk him away for the day.

"Hey, babe." He grinned and walked over and kissed me. "What are you doing here? Where are the twins?"

"They're with Tilly." I smiled, grabbing his tie and pulling him closer to me. "I'm here to give you another birthday present."

"Is that so?"

"Yes. So, come with me. Nico is downstairs waiting with the car."

"Can you give me about thirty minutes? I'm in the middle of finishing something."

"No, she can not." Chase smiled, entering Charlie's office. "I'll finish it. You go and enjoy the rest of your birthday."

"What are you up to?" Charlie smirked.

"You'll see. Come on."

We climbed into the back of the car.

"Good afternoon, Mr. Stone," Nico said.

"Good afternoon, Nico. Where are you taking us?"

"That's up to Marley to tell you, sir."

"He's right. It is up to me, and I'm not telling you until we get there." I smiled, kissing his cheek.

Nico pulled up to the Lowell Hotel, climbed out, and opened the door.

"The Lowell Hotel?" Charlie smiled.

"Happy Birthday. You have been invited to spend the entire afternoon and night with me, your girlfriend, in the luxurious Manhattan Suite, housing two fireplaces that will keep us warm on this cold day."

"You mean just the two of us?" He wiggled his finger. "Just us? No children?"

"No children, babe. Just you and me and a whole lot of sex." I grinned.

"But the doctor hasn't cleared you yet," he said as we entered the lobby.

"I called Dr. Gregario earlier in the week. He said it's fine as long as we don't behave like wild animals."

"Ha." He chuckled.

The bellman brought our bags up to the suite, and I grabbed Charlie's hand when he went to tip him.

"This is your day, and everything is on me," I said, pulling out some cash.

"I can't believe you did this. You are truly a romantic, Miss Monroe." His lips met mine.

"Well, I really wanted to take you somewhere warm, but I don't think it's a good idea to travel yet. Besides, I wanted you all to myself." My arms tightened around his neck.

"Is Tilly going to be okay with the twins alone?"

I could sense the worry in his voice.

"Penelope and Olivia are spending the night to help. The twins are in good hands between their nanny and godparents. Besides, if anything were to happen, we could be home in a flash. Now, let's go change into the white robes the hotel has provided for us."

"For what? I'd rather fuck you naked." He grinned.

"We aren't having sex yet." I led him to the bedroom.

"Why not?"

"Because I've arranged for a couple's massage. They'll be here any moment."

"Oh. Well, you know I have magic hands. I'd be more than happy to massage that sexy body for you." A smirk crossed his lips.

"Good things come to those who wait." I tossed the robe at him.

Chapter Thirty-Four

MARLEY

"Thank you very much. We enjoyed those massages. Didn't we, babe?" I glanced at Charlie.

"We sure did. Thank you." He smiled. "Now, can we——"

"Shush." I placed my finger on his lips. "Now, we're going down to Jacques Bar for a birthday drink."

"Why? We can have a birthday drink up here. I already scoped out the bar area."

"Charlie?" I cocked my head.

"Alright, babe. A birthday drink down at the bar sounds wonderful." He kissed my lips and got dressed.

We sat down at the bar, had a couple of drinks, and talked until a text came through that our dinner was ready in our room.

"We have to go. Come on." I stood up and grabbed Charlie's hand.

"Babe, I'm not done with my scotch yet."

"Doesn't matter. Bring it up to the room."

"Why are you in such a hurry to get back to the—ah, I know why." A big grin crossed his face as we stepped into the elevator.

Poor guy. He thought we were having sex the second we got up there. Just a bit longer, and then I'd let him have all the sex he wanted.

I unlocked the door to the room and when we stepped inside, I heard Charlie take in a sharp breath.

"What is all this?"

"A quiet and romantic birthday dinner for two." I smiled, kissing his cheek.

"You've thought of everything, haven't you?" he asked.

"Just about."

The dining table was laced with white cloth and fine white China that sat upon it. Candles flickered on the table, giving the room a romantic atmosphere. A bottle of the hotel's finest champagne sat in an ice bucket while a four-course meal graced the rest of the table, and the fireplace was glowing with a roaring fire.

"Look at all this." A smile crossed his lips. "I can't believe you did this for me."

"Why? I love you. And don't forget I'm an event planner. Planning special occasions is my specialty."

"I love you so damn much, Marley."

"I love you too, Charlie. Let's eat."

I was getting somewhat nervous because I was about to propose to him. What if he changed his mind about wanting to marry me? After we ate the delicious meal the hotel prepared for us, it was time to light the candles on the cake.

"Stay there. I'll be right back." I smiled as I stood up and went into the bedroom.

A beautiful buttercream cake decorated with a man in

a suit sitting on a couch holding a video game controller sat on the dresser, ready to be lit. After lighting the candles, I picked up the cake and sang my way back to the living area.

> "Happy birthday to you.
> Happy birthday to you.
> Happy birthday, dear Charlie.
> Happy birthday to you."

"Oh my God." He grinned when I set the cake down in front of him. "I love it."

I took in a long, deep breath, my heart pounding out of my chest and grabbed his hand.

"Happy birthday, my love. Charlie," I looked up at the ceiling to prevent the tears from falling, "I love you so much. I never thought I could love anyone like I love you and our babies. Once again, my entire life changed in the blink of an eye, but this time, it was a happy and welcomed change. You've taught me how to love. You're that ray of sunshine that pops up when I'm having a bad day. The minute I see you, my day gets brighter. I'm a little crazy. I know that. And I thank you for putting up with my craziness. I know I can be a handful at times, but you're mine, and you're mine to keep forever. I can't imagine my life without you. Will you marry me, Mr. Charles Stone?"

"Marley, are you serious?"

"Um, yeah." My brows furrowed.

"God, this is not what I was expecting."

Oh shit. Oh shit. Oh shit.

He brought his hands up and cupped my face.

"I love you so much, Marley. I can't believe this. I've wanted for so long to—"

"Give me this?" I reached into my back pocket and pulled out the engagement ring he'd bought me.

~

CHARLIE

I stared at the ring she held and then at her.

"You knew?"

"Yeah. I found it in your drawer. Well, actually, when the movers went to take your T-shirts out of the drawer, the box fell onto the floor. I felt so bad because I know I crushed you that night with all that gibberish bullshit talk about marriage. I'm so sorry, Charlie. I kept waiting for you to ask me, but you didn't, and then the twins were born early, and our life was chaos. It is still chaos, but I wasn't waiting for you anymore. I had to right my wrong. And what better time or way to do it than here with just us, on your birthday."

"Marley, yes. I will marry you." I grinned as I took the ring and slipped it on her finger. "You have no idea how happy this makes me." He stood up, took me in his arms, and spun me around, kissing my lips. "I can't imagine my life without you in it, and just for the record, you're mine forever, too. There's no way in hell I'm ever letting you go. And there's no way in hell I'm waiting any longer to take you to bed."

"Okay." She grinned. "Take me away, fiancé. But can we do it my way?"

"Any way you want, babe. Just name it."

"I want to turn off all the lights, spread out that big furry blanket over there in the corner, and make love in front of the warm fire."

"Your wish is my command." I set her down.

While she went to grab the pillows from the bed, I

spread out the large, furry blanket in front of the fireplace. When I looked up, she was standing there, completely naked, with two pillows covering her.

"Damn." I smiled as my cock instantly rose. Grabbing her hand, I pulled her down on the floor. "Babe, I don't have a condom on me."

"It's okay. Just pull out." Her lips met mine.

I thrust inside her slowly, listening to each pleasurable sound escape her lips. It felt so good to be buried inside her again as her warmth enveloped my cock. We needed to take it easy for now. I didn't want to risk hurting her. She let out a long moan as her body shook with ecstasy, causing my cock to spasm. I quickly pulled out and exploded all over the front of her.

"That's so hot," she moaned. "You need to do that more often."

"Anything you say." I smiled, leaning down and kissing her lips.

I got up and went to the bathroom to get some tissues. After we cleaned ourselves up, we lay on the blanket and stared at the peaceful fire.

"I miss the twins," I said.

"Me too." Her lips touched my chest before she got up and grabbed her phone. "Let's call and see how they are."

She dialed Tilly and put the phone on speaker. When Tilly answered, all we heard was screaming.

"Hey, Marley."

"Tilly, is everything okay?" she asked.

"Yeah. The twins want to be held non-stop. They aren't taking no for an answer."

"Are Penelope and Olivia holding up okay?" I asked.

"Olivia's passed out on the couch. The crying was stressing her out, so she drank a bottle of wine. Penelope's been a big help."

"Okay. We have to go. See you tomorrow. Bye, Tilly," Marley said and abruptly ended the call. "What was it that you said about missing the twins?" She cocked her head.

"I never said that. Nope. This, right here, is what I've missed."

"Good answer. Me too." She lay in my arms and lay her head on my chest.

Chapter Thirty-Five

CHARLIE

I had the best weekend and birthday of my life. One night spent alone with my sexy fiancée was more than I could have asked for. I'd spent most of yesterday hungover from the birthday bash Chase and Lila threw me. But I had to quickly sober up because Marley's father and Miranda were coming over for dinner. They were thrilled about our engagement and celebrated with us.

"Did you and Marley set a wedding date yet?" Chase asked.

"We did." I smiled, leaning back in my office chair. "We're getting married in five months."

"Five months? It took Lila and I a year and a half to plan our wedding. How the hell are you two doing it in five months?"

"She told me she has it covered and not to worry. Don't forget she's an event planner, which brings me to something I want to talk to you about."

"Okay. What is it?"

"For a wedding gift, I want to buy Marley a building

for her event planning business, filled with staff and everything she needs."

"Is she planning on doing events again? I figured with the twins, she wouldn't."

"Yeah, she's planning on it. She wanted to wait until the twins were at least six months old before taking on any new clients."

"I think you should talk to her first, Charlie."

"I plan on it." I smiled. "I'm going to call Grant and have him start looking for the perfect building for her."

"Since Lila got laid off from her administrative assistant job, maybe she can help Marley out."

"I'm sure Marley would love that. She and Lila are close."

～

Two Months Later

MARLEY

I stepped out of the dressing room and stood before my mom, Olivia, and Penelope, sitting there with champagne glasses.

"Marley. Oh, my God." Penelope walked over. "It's gorgeous on you."

"That's it, girl. That's the one." Olivia smiled, wiggling her finger.

"Mom?" I asked, noticing the tears in her eyes.

"It's perfect, Marley—absolutely perfect."

"And it's almost a perfect fit." Glenda, the sales associate, smiled. "We'll just need to take it in a little bit here." She grabbed my waist. "I have the perfect veil to match if you plan on wearing one."

"I really didn't think about a veil, but I'll try it on."

Tears sprung to my eyes when she placed the veil on my head.

"She'll take it." Olivia held up her champagne glass.

After finding the perfect wedding dress and having lunch, I headed home. When I walked through the door, it was abnormally quiet.

"Are they asleep?" I whispered to Tilly.

"Yes. They've been sleeping for about an hour."

I went upstairs and peeked at the twins sound asleep in their bassinets. Fifty percent of the time, they were truly angels. The other fifty percent, I was convinced they were the spawns of Satan. There was a loud bang at the door, which startled the twins and me. They began screaming, and I raced down the stairs to see who the hell it was. Upon opening the door, a burly man stood there in his brown UPS uniform, holding a large box.

"Really?" I cocked my head as Tilly ran up the stairs to quiet the twins. "Was it really necessary to bang on my door like that? Was it?"

"I need you to sign for this," he said, handing me his pad.

"And I need you to be respectful of parents with babies in the house. You woke up my twins with your loud banging!"

"What's going on here?" Charlie walked up the steps.

"This UPS man banged very loudly on the door and woke the twins up!"

"Ma'am, I needed your signature, and if I had lightly tapped, you wouldn't have heard me. I don't have all damn day to stand around waiting for someone to come to the door." He took the pad from me and walked away.

"What is your name?" I shouted.

Charlie picked up the box and stepped inside the house. "Let it go, babe. What is this?"

"I think it's our wedding invitations. Set it on the island in the kitchen. I'll open them after I help Tilly with the twins."

"I'll go help Tilly. You open the box and admire how beautiful the invitations look." He smiled as he kissed my lips.

"You're the best. Thank you."

"After I get the twins settled, I need to talk to you about something," he said.

"It sounds serious. Do I need to be worried?" I twisted my face.

"No." He chuckled. "Not at all. Order us some dinner, and we'll discuss it."

"What do you want?" I shouted as he walked up the stairs.

"Anything you do. You pick. You know what I like."

I ordered Thai food and asked Tilly if she would like to join us. She politely declined because she had a date with a guy she'd met a couple of weeks ago.

"You be careful. Guys cannot be trusted," Charlie told her.

"I will, Charlie."

"You call if you need us, Tilly. I mean it."

"I will." She looked at me over his shoulder, and I rolled my eyes."

After Tilly left, I hooked my arm around him and placed my hand on his chest.

"Practicing for when Ashley starts dating?" I asked.

"No. Why would you ask that? My daughter is never dating."

"Oh, okay, overprotective daddy."

"I'm serious, Marley. If I even see a boy lurking around here, I can't be held responsible for what I might do to him."

"And what are you going to do when she goes off to college at the age of eighteen?"

"She's not going off to college anywhere but here in New York, close to home."

"Don't be an asshole, Charlie."

"I'm not being an asshole. I'm merely protecting my daughter."

"Protecting her from men like you?" I smirked.

"Yes. From the men of how I used to be before you blew into my life and changed everything."

"And what about our son? Is he allowed to date?"

"Of course. He's a man. I don't have to worry about him."

"Ah, I see." I arched my brow. "And you don't think there's women out there waiting to get their claws into the young, handsome son of a billionaire?"

"Right. He's not allowed to date either. Let's go sit down and eat."

I placed the plates and the food on the table. Charlie and I sat down and ate while the twins were swinging in their swings.

"I want to invest in your event planning company."

"What?" My brows furrowed.

"It's my wedding gift to you. I want to invest a large sum, buy you a building with your name, and hire staff to help. You're a huge upcoming event planner that all the elite in New York will want to hire."

"Charlie, are you serious?"

"Very serious, babe. I've been in touch with Grant, and he has a couple of buildings to show us whenever you want to look at them. You said you would take on new clients when the twins reach six months. It's time to expand your business."

"I don't know what to say."

"Say yes." He grinned.

"Yes! Oh, yes." I jumped up from my seat and sat on his lap, wrapping my arms around his neck and planting kisses all over his face.

"I think we should take this upstairs." He smirked.

"What about the twins?"

"They're sound asleep in their swings."

"Let's go." I smiled, grabbing his hand.

We were halfway up the stairs when both children started crying. We stopped for a minute and listened, praying they'd stop. They didn't, and their cries grew louder.

"Well, it was a good idea for a hot second." Charlie sighed.

"Yep. It sure was." We turned back around and went down the stairs.

~

"I'M NERVOUS," I said to Penelope and Olivia.

"Don't be. He'll understand," Olivia said.

"You think?"

"Yes. It's what you want. You're the bride." Penelope smiled.

"But it's every father's dream to walk his daughter down the aisle."

"Times have changed. Traditions are out. Your dad is a grown man and will understand."

"Here he is now." Penelope stood up. "Good luck."

"Hey, sweetheart." My dad smiled, kissing my cheek. "Look at my precious grandchildren. Hi there, Ashton. Hi there, Ashley. It's your grandpa," he said, staring at them in their stroller.

"Thanks for meeting me here, Dad. Can I get you a coffee?"

"Sure. Just a regular black."

I held my finger up to Olivia. She knew exactly what to make my dad.

"So, what did you want to discuss with me?"

"I—I—"

"For fuck's sake." Olivia walked over and set my dad's coffee in front of him. "Marley loves you but doesn't want you to walk her down the aisle. She wants to carry the twins down with her, by herself, to Charlie."

"Really, sweetheart?" My dad cocked his head.

"Yeah, Dad. I'm so sorry." I shot Olivia a look.

"Nah, don't be. I think that's a wonderful idea. Does Charlie know you want to do this?"

"No. I want it to be a surprise. I'm not even showing him what the kids will wear."

"I love the idea, and so will he." My dad smiled.

Chapter Thirty-Six

CHARLIE

Marley and I were getting married at the St. Regis Hotel with two hundred twenty guests. Her two stepbrothers were flying in, and I couldn't wait to meet them.

I stood in front of the elegant floral archway with my hands folded, staring at the seated guests who came to celebrate our marriage.

"You look nervous," Chase said.

"I'm not nervous."

"Admit it. You are."

"Fine. Maybe a little."

"Don't be, Charlie. All that will disappear once you see your bride walk down that aisle." He patted my back.

"Where are the twins?" I asked.

"I don't know." He shrugged.

"Marley's mom was supposed to have them sit with her and Peter."

The music started to play, and the bridesmaids slowly walked down one by one.

When Olivia reached the end of the aisle, I looked at her.

"Where are the twins?"

"Don't worry. They're fine," she spoke through gritted teeth.

The bridal march began to play, and when I looked up, I saw Marley standing at the top of the aisle, holding Ashley in one arm and Ashton in the other. Tears filled my eyes as she slowly walked down the aisle, looking as gorgeous as ever.

"Wow," Chase whispered.

When she approached, a tear fell down my cheek. Ashley held her arms out to me, and I took her.

"You are so beautiful." I smiled at Marley.

"And you're so handsome. They're going to stay up here with us until we exchange our rings."

"I love that idea. Thank you."

I stood next to Marley with Ashley in my arms. Marley held Ashton while the minister said a few words. When it was time to exchange the rings, Penelope and Olivia stepped up and took the children from us. We turned to each other, said our heartfelt vows, and exchanged rings.

"I now pronounce you husband and wife. You may kiss your beautiful bride, Charlie."

Everyone clapped and whistled as I wrapped my arm around Marley's waist, dipped her, and kissed her as hard as I could.

"Hello, Mrs. Stone." I smiled.

"Hello, my husband."

We had a beautiful reception filled with our family and friends. Marley and I both made some of the decisions regarding the wedding preparations, but she had outdone herself, and I was so proud of her.

"Charlie, congratulations to you and your new bride." Loretta Stansfield smiled.

"Thank you, Loretta."

"The wedding is absolutely beautiful. May I ask who your event planner was?"

"That would be my wife." I smiled, hooking my arm around Marley's waist. "She's an event planner."

"Is that so? Well, my daughter just got engaged, and I would love to sit down and talk to you when you return from your honeymoon."

"I would love that." Marley smiled.

"Excellent. If you give me your phone number, I'll text you mine, and you can call me when you get back."

Marley rattled off her phone number while Loretta put it in her phone.

"Look at that. The Stansfield wedding will be huge." I smiled.

"I don't want to think about anyone's wedding but ours. Let's go cut the cake, husband."

"I'm right with you, wife. God, I love calling you that." A grin crossed my face.

～

Six Months Later

IT WAS hard to believe the twins would be one year old, and Marley and I had been married six months already. After a long day at work, I walked through the door, and the kids weren't the only ones screaming.

"No. You listen to me, you incompetent jackass! Those goddamn statues better be delivered to the address I sent you by Monday afternoon. I don't care if you have to drive to the Hamptons to get them yourself. You made a promise, and you're going to follow through, or I swear to God, I will hunt you down myself, cut off your balls, and feed them to your dog!" Marley shouted. "Thank you. I knew you would make things right. Goodbye, Chuck."

I walked over and picked up the kids. "Remind me never to make you angry." I smirked at Marley. "What has Chuck done now?"

"He's trying to say there was a mix-up on the order for the statues for the Garrison party." She placed her hand on her forehead.

"And what is wrong with these two?" My brow arched as I handed her Ashton.

"They were fighting over a toy, and Ashley hit Ashton in the head with her baby doll."

"Did my perfect angel hit her brother?" I hugged her tight. "That wasn't very nice. Did you apologize to your brother?"

"Dada." She placed her hand on my cheek. "Dada." She scrunched her nose like Marley always did. She was the spitting image of her.

"Look at that. She's already a manipulator," Marley said.

"She is her mother's daughter." The corners of my mouth curved upward.

"You will pay dearly for that remark, Mr. Stone."

"Promise?" I leaned in and kissed her lips.

"Oh, yes. I totally promise."

"I'm looking forward to it." I winked.

After dinner and giving the twins a bath, Marley and I put them to bed, but not without a fight from them.

"I love those kids so much, but sometimes—"

"You think they're the spawns of Satan?" Marley smirked.

"You know, babe. You really shouldn't say that about

our children." I walked into the bathroom to brush my teeth.

"Ha, okay. You think it too, and don't lie." She pointed at me with her hairbrush.

"Marley, I would never think—who the hell am I kidding?" I shook my head. When I was finished in the bathroom, I turned off the light and climbed into bed. "I know we've never discussed it, but—"

"No," she said.

"You didn't let me finish."

"I already know what you're going to ask me. You want to know if I want more kids. The answer is no. We have a son and a daughter, and I think we're the perfect family of four."

I let out a sigh of relief. "I completely agree with you." I hooked my arm around her as she snuggled into me.

"Since we're both in agreement, I'm not going to spend the rest of my life on birth control. So, I'll call the doctor and make an appointment for your vasectomy." She patted my chest.

"Now, hold on a second. Who said anything about a vasectomy?"

"You're right. I'm stopping my shots, and we'll use condoms until I reach menopause and can't get pregnant."

We heard Ashton start to cry through the monitor. Turning our heads, we stared at him, pulling himself up and standing in his crib. His cries became shrieks, which woke Ashley up.

"Parent duty calls," Marley said, climbing out of bed.

We went up to the nursery. I held Ashton while Marley took Ashley from her crib and tried to soothe her. As I sat down in the rocker to rock my son, he screamed louder.

"I don't know why they're crying like this," Marley said.

"It could be their ears again. Maybe you should get the Tylenol out."

"Tilly said they were very crabby all day, so you're probably right. Here." She handed me Ashley. "I'll be right back."

As I held both screaming kids in my arms, I rocked back and forth until Marley returned with the Tylenol. After giving each a dose, we paced around the room with them for over an hour until they finally fell asleep. We lay them down in their cribs, and I hooked my arm around Marley as we walked out of the nursery.

"Call that doctor tomorrow and make the appointment," I said.

"Oh, I am. You don't have to worry about that." She lay her head on my shoulder.

Chapter Thirty-Seven

FOUR YEARS LATER

MARLEY

Charlie and I spent the day in Central Park and had a picnic with the kids.

"This is nice." I smiled as I lay my head in Charlie's lap while the twins chased each other and played.

"It sure is. I can't believe they're going to be five years old in a few weeks," he said.

"I can't either. They're growing so fast."

"Do you regret not having any more kids?" he asked.

"I will admit there was a time or two where I started to get baby fever, but then the twins would start fighting and screaming, and that feeling flew out the window."

"Same for me." He chuckled.

"Before you know it, they'll be teenagers and then off to college."

"I don't even want to think about that, Marley. I won't ever be ready to let them go."

"Daddy, Ashton hit me." Ashley ran over and cried.

"No, I didn't. She's lying," Ashton said.

"You're lying!" Ashley pushed him down.

Ashton started crying. I lifted my head and looked at Charlie.

"You were saying?" I arched my brow.

"Right. Maybe college can't come fast enough."

We calmed the children down by giving them a snack before packing up and heading home. As we walked through the park, I stopped when I saw a familiar face sitting on a bench.

"Charlie, is that—"

"Yep. What's he doing back in New York?"

I took hold of Ashley's and Ashton's hands and knelt before them.

"Kids, do you want to play a game?"

"Yeah!" Both children exclaimed.

"See that man sitting on the bench by himself?"

"Marley, don't," Charlie spoke.

"Yeah, Mommy," both children said.

"I want you to run over to him and yell 'Daddy.'"

"Marley—"

"Shush, Charlie. Go on, you two. We'll be right behind you."

"What the hell are you doing?" Charlie whispered.

"Having a little fun." I grinned.

Ashley and Ashton ran up to Troy. The look on his face was priceless, and I wished I had my phone out.

"Marley?" His eyes widened as I approached him. "What the hell?"

"Language in front of your children." I smiled. "I'm happy you're back in New York. Now, we can go to court for all the back child support you owe for the last five years."

"These are not my kids!"

"Daddy, Daddy, Daddy!" Ashton jumped up and down.

"Stop that!" Troy stood up. "Listen, Marley. I'm broke. I have nothing to give you. You look very familiar to me." He looked at Charlie.

"Chicago airport," Charlie said. "About six years ago."

"That's right. You were the guy sitting next to her in the airport and the plane."

"Listen, Troy. The twins are mine, not yours. Marley was just playing around with you. And I will admit that what you did by lying to her and telling her you were single to get her to sleep with you was wrong. Not to mention the crap you pulled with your ex."

"They're not mine?" Troy asked.

"Do you not understand English?" I cocked my head.

"Wow, Marley. Who the hell tells a man they're the father when he's not? That's just pure evil." He shook his head, walked away, and then turned around. "You are one evil woman."

"You're no fun," I pouted, glancing at Charlie.

"Let it go, babe. Let it go." He hooked his arm around me and kissed the side of my head.

"Daddy, Mommy's not evil," Ashley said.

"She can be when she wants to be, sweetheart."

"You are going to pay for that, Stone." I smacked his chest.

"Promise?"

Twelve Years Later

MARLEY

When they graduated, Charlie and I took the twins to Paris for the summer. They were planning on backpacking through Europe together, and I was all for it since I'd done it when I was their age, but Charlie wouldn't let them. He had planned this trip well in advance, which allowed me not to schedule any major events while we were gone. While we were sitting on the patio of the beautiful home he rented us for the summer, sipping wine and eating cheese and crackers, Ashley walked out holding a boy's hand. I immediately placed my hand on Charlie's arm to keep him calm.

"Mom. Dad. I'd like you to meet Luca. Luca, these are my parents, Charlie and Marley."

"It's so nice to meet you. Ashley has told me so much about the two of you."

"How old are you?" Charlie asked.

"Dad!"

"I'm seventeen, sir. Can I just say that I'm a huge fan of your video games?"

"Are you now?"

"Yes."

"Luca is a genius at coding and developed his own game, Daddy."

"You did?" Charlie tipped the glass to his lips.

"It's really no big deal. I just did it for fun."

"And how and when did the two of you meet?" Charlie asked.

"I met Luca at the fruit stand. His parents own it. I went to pick up an orange, and they all started falling." Ashley smiled. "We're going out. Come on, Luca."

"Where are you going?" Charlie asked.

"To dinner."

"I will make sure to have your daughter home before her curfew," Luca said.

"I'll be watching," Charlie spoke.

"Mom!"

"Go on and have a nice dinner." I smiled. "What is wrong with you?" I cocked my head at Charlie.

"You don't see anything wrong here, babe?"

"No. She's almost eighteen and is interested in a boy in Paris. I think it's cute. And he seems like a really nice boy. Besides, you should be flattered."

"Flattered? Why should I be flattered?"

"Because she picked a boy who reminds her of her Daddy." I grinned.

"I don't trust him."

"You never trust any of the guys she's dated the past couple of years."

"Exactly! And look at what they did to her."

"They did nothing to her." I laughed. "She broke it off with them because they weren't good enough for her."

"Hey, you two." Ashton walked out, looking as handsome as ever. "I'm going out."

"Where are you going, son?" Charlie asked.

"I met this girl the other day, and we've been talking. I'm taking her on a date. Can I borrow your credit card, Dad?"

"Sure, son." He reached into his wallet, pulled out his credit card, and handed it to Ashton. "Who is this girl?"

"She's great and so beautiful."

"Have a good time and be safe," Charlie said.

I sat there and glared at him.

"Oh, by the way. I saw you met Luca. He's a really great guy, Dad. You don't have to worry about him. I'll see you two later."

"Seriously?" I said to Charlie.

"What? He's a man. It's different when it comes to Ashley." He took out his phone and pulled up her location.

"Give me that." I grabbed his phone from his hand.

Epilogue

Six Years Later

CHARLIE

Six months after we returned from Paris, Luca moved to New York and attended Columbia with Ashley and Ashton. I wasn't happy when she told us, but I saw the way they looked at each other and knew they were meant to be together. Ashley sobbed on the plane the day we left Paris to return home and for days afterward. She was miserable, and I hated seeing her that way. I was impressed that Luca moved from his home and away from his family to be close to my daughter. Not just any man would do that unless he was in love.

The more I got to know him, the more I liked him. Marley loved him right off the bat, but it took me a little longer. I looked at the game he developed and saw he was on to something. While he attended Columbia, I brought him into my company as an intern. Considering he was my future son-in-law, I hired him full-time after he graduated.

On the other hand, Ashton was playing the field and refused to commit to anyone.

I walked into the suite at the Plaza Hotel, and tears filled my eyes when my daughter turned and looked at me. I couldn't believe the day had come when I'd give her away to another man. She was twenty-four years old, very strong and independent like her mother, and my marketing manager, who worked alongside her brother at Stone Game Ventures—the company they would run when I retired.

"Hi, Dad."

"God, look at you—my baby girl. You look so beautiful, sweetheart." I brought my hand up to her cheek. "You remind me so much of your mother."

"Thanks, Dad."

"It's time. Are you ready?"

"I'm more than ready. I can't wait to marry him, Daddy."

"I know the feeling, sweetheart." I held my arm out.

I stood at the top of the aisle, Ashley's arms wrapped around mine and slowly walked her to her future husband. After placing her hand in Luca's, I took a seat next to my beautiful wife.

"Are you okay?" Marley asked, squeezing my hand.

"I'm fine, babe." I smiled.

After the ceremony, and many pictures later, we went to the ballroom for the reception.

"You have outdone yourself with our daughter's wedding." I kissed Marley's lips.

"Thank you. Nothing but the best for her."

I walked over to the bar, where Ashton was getting a scotch.

"Hey, Dad. Want one?"

"Yes, son." I patted his back.

"Hi." A lovely young woman smiled at Ashton.

"Well, hello there, beautiful." He grinned. "Dad, I'll catch you later."

I inhaled a sharp breath and shook my head as I walked away and over to Marley.

"Who is that girl Ashton is talking to?" she asked.

"Just another casualty, babe. Just another casualty."

One Year Later

"I'LL MISS YOU." Marley wrapped her arms around my neck.

"I'll miss you too, babe. I'll be back in three days." I kissed her.

"It sucks you have to fly commercial." A smirk crossed her lips.

"Don't remind me. I can't believe the private jet isn't fixed yet." I sighed.

"You'll be fine. Ashton will be with you, which reminds me. Keep him in line, please."

"Trust me. I will. I'll see you when I get back. I love you so much." I hugged her tight.

"I love you too."

Our business trip went great. As we were sitting in the Chicago airport, it was announced that our flight was delayed due to severe storms.

"Great." I shook my head.

"Yeah. No kidding," Ashton spoke.

As we were both scrolling on our phones, a young woman sat in the empty seat next to Ashton.

"Yay! I can't believe I got upgraded to first class." She waved her boarding pass.

"That's nice," Ashton said, and I chuckled.

"I've never been in first class before."

"I'm sure you'll enjoy it." Ashton sighed.

He was in a mood, and I wasn't sure why. His phone rang.

"What do you want, Kristen? You know I'm on a business trip with my dad. Listen, I'm not discussing this now or ever. Great. You've saved me the trouble. Have a good day, Kristen, and lose my number."

I sat there, trying to mind my own business and ignore what I'd just heard.

"Trouble in paradise?" the young girl spoke.

"Um, no."

"It kind of sounded like your girlfriend broke up with you."

"First of all, she wasn't my girlfriend, and second, do you always listen in on other people's conversations?"

"No. But it's hard not to listen when there's screaming coming from the other end."

I leaned forward and stared at the young and beautiful woman.

"Excuse me. Do you live in New York?" I asked her.

"Yes, I do." She smiled.

"Dad." Ashton lightly smacked my arm.

"I'm going to get a coffee. Can you watch my bag and make sure nobody takes my seat?" she asked.

"Of course he will." I grinned.

"Thank you. Can I get either of you one?"

"I'm good. Thanks," I said.

"Since I'm watching your bag and seat, I'll have a medium Americano with an extra shot," Ashton said.

"Okay. I'll be right back."

"She's kind of annoying." Ashton looked at me. "Beautiful, but annoying."

"I'm going to head to the restroom, son," I said as I stood up.

"Okay, Dad."

I followed the young girl to Starbucks.

"Excuse me," I said. "Which seat are you sitting in?"

"Um, 3B." She glanced at her boarding pass.

"How would you like to switch seats?" I smiled. "I'm not really feeling the window seat today."

"Are you sure?" she asked.

"I'm positive." I smiled.

As I walked away, I heard they were starting to board our plane.

"Here's your coffee," the young woman said, handing the cup to Ashton.

He took a sip. "This is not an Americano."

"Are you sure? It says Americano on the cup," the young woman spoke.

"I know an Americano when I taste one, and this isn't it."

"Then the barista messed up. There's no need to act like a child about it."

"Excuse me?" Ashton cocked his head.

"By the way, you owe me eight dollars for the coffee," she said, and I chuckled.

"Eight dollars for this crap?"

"Pay her, son." I placed my hand on his shoulder with a smile.

She took the money from Ashton's hand, scanned her boarding pass, and walked ahead of us.

"I hope that woman isn't sitting anywhere near us," Ashton said.

I smiled all the way down the loading bridge to the plane. When Ashton reached his seat, he stopped in the aisle and stared at the young woman.

"Uh, you're sitting in my dad's seat."

"Your dad told me I could sit here. He wasn't feeling the window seat today."

The smile never left my face as he stared at me while I placed my bag in the overhead and took the seat behind him. A few moments later, a text came through from him.

"What the hell are you doing?"

"You've just met your future wife, son."

He immediately turned around and looked at me.

One Year Later

ANNA AND ASHTON married one year after meeting at the Chicago airport. Ashley was due to give birth to our first grandchild, a little girl, in a month, and Marley and I couldn't wait to become grandparents.

After saying goodbye to Anna and Ashton as they left for their two-week honeymoon in Aruba, I hooked my arm around my beautiful wife.

"Who would have thought our son would settle down." She smiled.

"I knew it the second Anna sat next to him at the airport. My God, babe. It was like you and me all those years ago."

"You did good, my love. We've waited for this day for a long time."

"Do you regret not having any more kids?" I asked.

"Nope. We did right by the twins, and now, we'll have a granddaughter to dote on and help raise. You know what the best part will be?"

"What?" I tenderly kissed her lips.

"We get to send her home." A bright smile graced her face.

"We do, don't we?" I smiled as we walked to the car.

"Yep." Marley popped her lips. "We've paid our dues and put in our time. Now, it's our children's turn to do the same."

"It sure is, babe. Have I told you how much I love you?"

"A few times." She smirked as we climbed into the back of the car.

"Well, when we get home, I'll show you just how much I love you."

"Promise, you bad boy?"

"Have I ever broken a promise to you?" I kissed her soft and beautiful lips.

Thank you for reading Baby Drama III! I hope you enjoyed it!

You can read Grant Roman's story in The Property Brokers.

Download Here

Adalyn Grant is New York's sought after interior designer. You can read her story in The Ring.

Download Here

Remember Morgan Ashley, the hacker Charlie called on to check out Troy? Stay tuned for her story coming in a brand new series!

I invite you to join my Sandi's Romance Readers Facebook Group, where we talk about books, romance, and more! Join the fun!

Newsletter
Website
Facebook
Instagram
FOLLOW ME ON AMAZON
TikTok
Bookbub
Goodreads

More Sizzling Romance

Looking for more romance reads about billionaires, second chances, and sports? Check out my other romance novels and escape to another world and from the daily grind of life – one book at a time.

Series:

Forever Series:
Forever Black (Forever, Book 1)
Forever You (Forever, Book 2)
Forever Us (Forever, Book 3)
Being Julia (Forever, Book 4)
Collin (Forever, Book 5)
A Forever Family (Forever, Book 6)
A Forever Christmas (Holiday short story)

Wyatt Brothers Series:
Love, Lust & A Millionaire (Wyatt Brothers, Book 1)
Love, Lust & Liam (Wyatt Brothers, Book 2)

A Millionaire's Love Series:
Lie Next to Me (A Millionaire's Love, Book 1)
When I Lie with You (A Millionaire's Love, Book 2)

Happened Series:
Then You Happened (Happened Series, Book 1)
Then We Happened (Happened Series, Book 2)

Redemption Series:
Carter Grayson (Redemption Series, Book 1)
Chase Calloway (Redemption Series, Book 2)
Jamieson Finn (Redemption Series, Book 3)
Damien Prescott (Redemption Series, Book 4)

Interview Series:
The Interview: New York & Los Angeles Part 1
The Interview: New York & Los Angeles Part 2

Love Series:
Love In Between (Love Series, Book 1)
The Upside of Love (Love Series, Book 2)

Wolfe Brothers Series:
Elijah Wolfe (Wolfe Brothers, Book 1)
Nathan Wolfe (Wolfe Brothers, Book 2)
Mason Wolfe (Wolfe Brothers, Book 3)

Kind Brothers Series:
One of a Kind (Kind Brothers Series, Book 1)
Two of a Kind (Kind Brothers Series, Book 2)
Three of a Kind (Kind Brothers Series, Book 3)
Four of a Kind (Kind Brothers Series, Book 4)
Five of a Kind (Kind Brothers Series, Book 5)
The Kind Brothers (Kind Brothers Series, Book 6)

Six of a Kind (Kind Brothers Series, Book 7)
Seven of a Kind (Kind Brothers Series, Book 8)
Eight of a Kind (Kind Brothers Series, Book 9)
Nine of a Kind (Kind Brothers Series, Book 10)
A Kind Wedding: Jackson & Georgia (Kind Brothers
Series, Book 11)
A Kind Wedding: Conner & Charlotte (Kind Brothers
Series, Book 12)
A Kind Wedding: Nathan & Sofia (Kind Brothers Series,
Book 13)
A Kind Wedding: Christian & Charleigh (Kind Brothers
Series, Book 14)
Ten of a Kind (Kind Brothers Series, Book 15)
Eleven of a Kind (Kind Brothers Series, Book 16)
Twelve of a Kind (Kind Brothers Series, Book 17)
Thirteen of a Kind (Kind Brothers Series, Book 18)
Fourteen of a Kind (Kind Brothers Series, Book 19)

One Night Series:
One Night In London
One Night In Paris

Broken Hearts Series:
Unspoken
A Beautiful Sight

Baby Drama Series:
Baby Drama
Baby Drama II
Baby Drama III

Standalone Books

The Billionaire's Christmas Baby

More Sizzling Romance

His Proposed Deal
The Secret He Holds
The Seduction of Alex Parker
Something About Lorelei
The Exception
Corporate Assets
The Negotiation
Defense
The Con Artist
#Delete
Behind His Lies
Perfectly You
The Escort
The Ring
The Donor
Rewind
Remembering You
When I'm With You
LOGAN (A Hockey Romance)
The Merger
Baby Drama
The Property Brokers

Printed in Dunstable, United Kingdom